Ola and the
Sea Wolf

Also by Barbara Cartland
in Large Print:

A Caretaker of Love
A Duke in Danger
From Hate to Love
A Kiss in Rome
Lights, Laughter and a Lady
The Love Puzzle
A Night of Gaiety
The Prude and the Prodigal
Secret Harbor
Secrets of the Heart
A Song of Love
The Taming of a Tigress

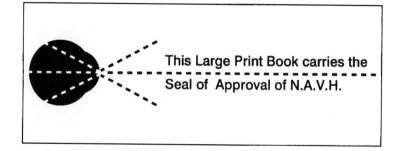

Barbara Cartland

Ola and the
Sea Wolf

Thorndike Press • Waterville, Maine

Published in 2002 by arrangement with
International Book Marketing Limited.

Thorndike Press Large Print Paperback Series.

The tree indicium is a trademark of Thorndike Press.

The text of this Large Print edition is unabridged.
Other aspects of the book may vary from the original edition.

Set in 16 pt. Plantin by Myrna S. Raven.

Printed in the United States on permanent paper.

Library of Congress Cataloging-in-Publication Data

Cartland, Barbara, 1902–
    Ola and the sea wolf / Barbara Cartland.
      p. cm.
    ISBN 0-7862-4248-5 (lg. print : sc : alk. paper)
    1. Large type books. I. Title.
  PR6005.A765 O43 2002
   823′.912—dc21   2002024550

Ola and the
Sea Wolf

Author's Note

The English exploring Europe in the Eighteenth Century travelled at considerable risk not only to their purses but to their lives, and it was not much better in the Nineteenth Century.

William Beckford, going to Venice, was warned: "Your route is sure to be very perilous . . . there lurk the most savage *banditti* in Europe."

The winding coast road to Italy at the foot of the Ligurian Alps was known to be beset by bandits, and the country roads in Germany were extremely dangerous.

Spain and Greece were even more perilous. In the Nineteenth Century the *Pallikares* were legendary mercenaries from the Albanian mountains. They were handsome and breathed fire and adventure, and the ladies of King Otto's Court found them very romantic. Travellers described them differently, if they lived to tell the tale!

CHAPTER ONE

1831

It was very quiet in the bar-room of The Three Bells, which was unusual.

Being close to the Harbour at Dover, it was usually filled with seamen and those repairing and victualling the ships.

But the thick fog outside seemed to penetrate even into the low-beamed room, and only the crackling of the logs in the open fireplace seemed to relieve the gloom.

The Landlord of The Three Bells found it difficult not to keep watching the door and hoping it would open. Then his eyes would go to his only customer, who was sitting in front of the log fire with his long legs outstretched.

He had not moved for some time, when he reached out to pour another glass from the bottle which stood beside him.

This made the Landlord anxious, not that the gentleman might be overindulging but because the bottle from which he was drinking, being of the best French Cognac, was the only one in the Inn.

It had been brought across the Channel by a seaman from whom he had bought it cheaply, considering its worth, and it was of a quality that was seldom demanded by the clientele of The Three Bells.

He looked at the gentleman and wondered who he was.

There was no doubt that he was of some social standing, and he had an authoritative air about him which had made the Proprietor greet him effusively on his arrival.

He supposed, for the gentleman was uncommunicative, that he owned one of the yachts in the Harbour and that it had been rendered immobile along with all the other shipping since the fog had closed in.

The gentleman raised the glass to his lips and as he did so the outside door was pushed open and someone came into the room.

To the Proprietor's surprise it was a woman, or rather, as he saw at a glance, a lady.

She was wearing a cloak trimmed with expensive fur but there was a tear in the fabric, and her hands, which were holding a leather case, were trembling.

For a moment she just stood looking round her as if she was a little dazed. Then as the Proprietor found his voice, saying respectfully: "Good-evening, Ma'am!" she turned to look at him and he saw that her very large eyes were wide and frightened.

"There . . . has been . . . an accident," she said a little incoherently.

"An accident, Ma'am?"

"Outside . . . at least . . . a little way down the . . . road. I saw . . . your . . . lights."

"I'll send some'un to help, Ma'am," the Proprietor said, "an' if ye'll come an' sit down by the fire, my man'll report to ye when he's found out what's a-happening."

As he spoke he turned and walked to a door which opened onto the back of the Inn.

"Joe! Are ye there?"

"Aye, Guv'," a voice replied.

"Then nip outside an' see if you can give a hand. There's a lady here says as how there's been a accident."

"Oi'll do that."

The Proprietor came from behind the bar to follow the lady, who was moving slowly, almost as if she was afraid of falling, towards the fireplace.

He pulled out an arm-chair for her which was opposite the one occupied by the gentleman, and as she sat down he said:

"I'm sure, Ma'am, ye'd like a drink after what must have been a nasty experience."

"It is very . . . foggy."

11

"Yes, I knows, Ma'am, it's been like this all day. Now, what can I get ye? We've got just about everything ye might fancy."

"Would it be . . . possible to have a . . . cup of tea?"

The Proprietor hesitated.

He was thinking that the tea that his wife drank, which was coarse and strong, would hardly be to the liking of anyone so elegant and delicate as the lady appeared to be.

Then, without moving, the gentleman on the other side of the fireplace remarked:

"If you have been in an accident, you had best have a glass of brandy. What I have here is quite drinkable."

The lady looked at him and after a moment's hesitation replied:

"That is very . . . kind of you . . . Sir . . . but I would . . . prefer tea or coffee."

"In this sort of place I would not recommend either!" the gentleman replied in a contemptuous voice.

As if she felt he was being unnecessarily rude to the Proprietor, the lady said quickly:

"Perhaps a glass of . . . Madeira would be easier . . . but only a half a glass, if you please."

"I'll get it for ye immediate!" the Proprietor replied.

Pleased that the choice had been settled,

he went behind the bar.

The lady was conscious that the gentleman opposite her was regarding her through half-closed eyes.

She thought he seemed a disagreeable type of person, and because she felt a little embarrassed she set the leather case she carried down on the floor at her feet and occupied herself in taking off her gloves.

The Proprietor returned with the Madeira in a small glass.

"This be a good quality, Ma'am," he said, "and I hope ye enjoys it."

"I am sure I shall," the lady replied, "and thank you very much."

She took the glass from him and said in a tone that was urgent:

"Can you tell me when there will be a ship . . . leaving for . . . France?"

"That's a question I can't answer, Ma'am," the Proprietor replied. "Nothing's moved out o' the Harbour all day. In fact, I were a-saying a short while ago that 'tis the worst fog I've known for twenty years or more!"

"There must be . . . one, perhaps very early . . . tomorrow morning?"

Now there was no doubt of the urgency in her tone.

The Proprietor shook his head.

"Depends on th' wind, Ma'am. If the wind gets up in th' night, then the *Britannia* should reach here from Calais an' make the return journey sometime in th' afternoon."

The lady gave a little cry of horror.

"Not until the afternoon? But surely there will be a ship leaving in the morning?"

"They be stuck t'other side of th' Channel," the Proprietor replied.

"B-but I must leave . . . I have to leave as . . . early as possible."

The Proprietor did not reply and she said almost frantically:

"Perhaps there would be a fishing-vessel that would take me? I believe they go out at dawn?"

"Not when th' weather's like this, Ma'am. An' anyway they fishes along th' shore."

The information he had given the lady obviously agitated her.

He could see an expression on her face that was almost one of desperation, and she was twisting her long fingers together almost as if they were like a problem which she had to solve.

"I'll tell ye what I'll do, Ma'am," the Proprietor said, as if in an effort to comfort her. "When Joe gets back t' tell ye about th' accident, I'll send him down to th' Quay to ask th' Harbour-Master if he can think of a way to help ye."

The lady's eyes seemed to brighten.

"Would you really do that? It is very kind of you. Please tell Joe I shall be pleased to reward him for his services."

"Thank ye, Ma'am. He should be back here soon. I wonder what's a-keeping him."

As he spoke, he walked away to open the outer door. As he did so, the fog seemed to swirl into the room like a grey cloud.

The door shut behind him and the lady sat back in her chair and shut her eyes.

She felt as if she must faint from the horror of it all. Then a voice at the other side of the fireplace said sharply:

"Drink your Madeira!"

It was too much of an effort to reply, and she felt a darkness like the fog creeping over her, and despite the fire she suddenly felt very cold.

Then somebody put a hand behind her head, there was a glass held to her lips, and almost despite herself she swallowed.

She felt a fiery liquid coursing down her throat and into her body, and almost instantly the darkness faded and it was easier to breathe.

"Another sip of brandy," the voice said sharply.

Although she wanted to protest, she

15

obeyed because for the moment she was not capable of arguing.

The second sip was even more effective than the first, and she opened her eyes to find the gentleman bending over her.

Now that she could see him more clearly, she realised that he was in fact exceedingly handsome, except that there was what she could only describe as a "darkness" about his eyes and a cynicism in the deeply etched lines on his face.

He would, she thought, have persuaded her to drink even more of the wine, but she put up her hands in protest.

"Please," she pleaded, "I am . . . all right now . . . and I could not . . . drink any . . . more."

As if he realised she was speaking the truth, the gentleman moved to stand with his back to the fire. He was, the lady noted, so tall that his head almost touched the heavy ships' beams that supported the ceiling.

He did not speak and after a moment she said in a nervous little voice:

"Thank you for . . . being . . . so kind. The . . . accident . . . upset me."

"Whoever was driving you must have been a fool to take his horses out in this weather."

"It was . . . my fault."

16

As she spoke, the outer door opened and the Proprietor came back into the room.

He looked towards the lady but he did not speak. Instead, he held the door open, and a moment later two men appeared, carrying between them a man who was obviously unconscious.

There was blood on his face from an open wound on his forehead and his clothes were covered in mud as if he had fallen violently onto the dirty roadway.

"Upstairs and put him in th' Guest-Room, Joe," the Proprietor was saying, "then see if ye can get hold of th' Doctor. Ye'll find him at Th' Crown and Anchor. He be always there at this time o' night."

"Right ye are, Guv'," Joe replied.

His voice had become almost inaudible as he and the other man with their burden disappeared through the door at the side of the bar which led to the other part of the Inn.

The Landlord shut the outer door and followed them, and they could hear his voice admonishing the men to be careful as they negotiated the stairs which led to the first floor.

At the first sight of the injured man the lady had sprung from her chair to stand staring at his prostrate body until he was out of sight.

Now she said almost as if she spoke to herself:

"There . . . must be a ship . . . there must!"

The gentleman, standing in front of the fire, turned to look at her and realised that she appeared to have forgotten his presence.

"Is it your husband that you are so anxious to run away from?" he enquired. "Or your Guardian?"

He spoke mockingly and he thought the latter was the more likely.

The man who had been injured was obviously in his forties, but he judged the woman beside him to be little more than a girl of eighteen.

She turned her head at the sound of his voice, and now that he could see her more clearly in the light from the fire, he realised that her pointed face was extremely attractive and the lashes that fringed her eyes were long and dark.

It was an arresting face, but there was no admiration in his eyes as he said, almost as if he jeered at her:

"Surely it must be one or the other!"

Before she answered him she sat down again in the chair. Then she said:

"He is . . . neither! He is a man who is . . . abducting me and I have to . . . escape from him!"

"Abducting you? Then surely it is quite easy. You can hire a post-chaise to take you back to wherever you have come from."

The lady shook her head.

"That is . . . impossible!"

"Then suppose you explain! I am not asking out of idle curiosity, but I might — although I am not committing myself — be able to help you."

The expression on the lady's face altered immediately.

"Oh . . . could you help me . . . could you really? Do you mean you could find me a ship . . . or perhaps . . ."

She hesitated a moment; then, as if she was impressed by the manner in which the gentleman was dressed, she finished her sentence by saying:

". . . You have . . . one of your . . . own?"

"I am asking the questions," the gentleman replied. "Why are you running away, and from whom?"

The lady drew in her breath before she answered:

"From my . . . Stepmother!"

The gentleman raised his eye-brows. It was an answer he had not expected. Then he said:

"Perhaps before we go any further we should introduce ourselves. I am the

19

Marquis of Elvington . . ."

Before he could say any more, the lady gave a little cry and said:

"I have heard of you! You are famous, and of course you have a yacht. That is why you are here. Oh, please . . . please, take me to France! I have to get away . . . and quickly!"

"From the man upstairs who is abducting you?"

"Yes . . . I never imagined . . . I never dreamt for one . . . moment that he would behave . . ."

Her words seemed to fail and she made a kind of helpless gesture with her hands that was somehow pathetic.

"I am waiting for you to tell me your name," the Marquis said.

"It is . . . Ola Milford. My father was Lord Milford and we live near Canterbury."

"I seem to have heard the name," the Marquis said cautiously.

"Papa did not often go to London. He preferred being in the country and he was not well for two years before he . . . died."

"You say it is your Stepmother from whom you are running away?"

"Yes . . . I cannot . . . stay with her any . . . longer! It is . . . impossible!"

"Why?"

"She hates me! She makes my life an ab-

20

solute misery! She is my Guardian but she will not give me any of the money that Papa left me. It is mine, but I do not have the . . . handling of it until I am . . . twenty-one or am . . . married."

"That should not be too difficult," the Marquis remarked cynically.

"You do not understand!" Ola Milford replied. "My Stepmother, who married Papa three years ago when he was so unhappy after Mama's death, is . . . jealous of me."

She said the word a little hesitatingly, as if she felt uncomfortable at telling the truth. Then she continued:

"She keeps saying she wishes to be rid of me . . . but she prevents me from going anywhere . . . and if a gentleman comes to the house she will not let me talk to him . . . I think actually she wants to get married again herself."

"Surely there are other relations with whom you could live?" the Marquis suggested.

"I have thought of that, but when I suggested it," Ola replied, "my Stepmother refused to contemplate such an idea because she thought I would take my money with me."

She gave a deep sigh.

"It is my money that is at the bottom of all

the trouble, both with my Stepmother and with my . . . cousin . . . upstairs."

She looked upwards as she spoke and the Marquis saw her give a little shiver.

"Your *cousin?*" he questioned. "How does he come into it?"

"I was desperate . . . absolutely desperate at the way my Stepmother was . . . treating me. You cannot know what it is like to live with hatred . . . and incessant faultfinding."

"I can imagine," the Marquis replied. "Go on!"

"I decided there was only one thing I could do and that was to go back to the Convent near Paris where I was educated, and become a Nun, or else, as my Stepmother has suggested so often, a cocotte!"

The Marquis was visibly startled.

"A what?" he questioned. "Do you know what you are saying?"

"I do not know . . . exactly what it entails," Ola admitted, "but if she has said it once she has said it a thousand times: 'With hair like yours, you should be a cocotte and that is about all you are suited for!'"

As if to demonstrate what she was saying, she pushed back the hood of her cloak which she had worn ever since she came into the Inn.

Suddenly it seemed as if the flames from

the fire had transferred themselves to the chair opposite the Marquis.

He had seen many women with red hair but never one whose colour was so vivid or indeed so beautiful as that of the girl opposite him.

Because her hair had been covered by the fur-lined hood for some time, it was for the moment flat on her small head.

Then, after she had unfastened her cape at the neck and let it fall down behind her in the chair, she ran her fingers through her hair and it seemed almost to come alive.

It glinted as it caught the light and its vivid hue made her skin seem almost dazzlingly white.

'It is not surprising,' he thought, 'that any woman, especially a Stepmother, would wish to be rid of a potential rival whose appearance is not only unusual but spectacular!'

The Marquis felt that Ola was waiting for him to comment and he said drily:

"I cannot commend either suggestion to you. You must think of an alternative."

"I have thought and thought," Ola replied, "but what can I do if Step-Mama will give me no money and will not permit me to live anywhere except with her?"

"I see there is some difficulty about that."

"Of course there are difficulties!" she retorted. "I assure you I do not intend to do anything stupid; I just wish to stay with the Nuns and discuss my future with the Mother-Superior who has always been very kind to me."

She paused before she added:

"Perhaps I should take the veil. It would certainly prevent me from being bullied and persecuted as I have been these last years."

"I am surprised at your being so faint-hearted."

As if the Marquis had stung her, not only with his words but with what she thought was contempt in his voice, Ola sat upright.

"It is all very well for you to talk," she replied. "You have no idea what it is like to be slapped and pinched and even occasionally beaten when Step-Mama has a whip in her hand."

She drew in her breath before she went on:

"The servants are not allowed to obey my orders or to bring me food if she says I am not to have it. When visitors come to the house I am sent to my bedroom, and if they are friends of Mama's I am locked in so that I cannot talk to them."

She gave a deep sigh.

"I have tried to defy her, I have tried to assert myself for two years, and now the only way I can remain sane is to run away."

"So you have decided to go to France," the Marquis said. "Where does your escort come in?"

He saw Ola's lips tighten and she replied in a very different voice:

"He has behaved despicably, utterly and completely despicably! I did not believe that any man could be so treacherous!"

"What did he do?"

"He is my cousin, but I always thought that although he is old, he was kind. When he came to stay, because I thought Step-Mama fancied him, I left a note in his bedroom begging him to see me alone, and he agreed."

She glanced at the Marquis to see if he was listening, then she continued:

"He gave me a perceptible nod when he came down to dinner, and after I had been sent to bed early so that Step-Mama could talk to him, I managed to jump from the balcony to his room next door. It was a dangerous thing to do, but I managed it."

"Was he surprised?"

"I think he thought I would come to him, but he did not know I was locked in my room at night."

The Marquis looked surprised and Ola said scathingly:

"That was to prevent me from finding out what my Stepmother was up to when she had her friends to stay. She need not have worried. I was not interested. I only . . . hate her!"

"I expect with hair that colour you are overemotional anyway!" the Marquis said.

"Any more references to my hair either from you or from anybody else," Ola snapped, "and I shall either cut it all off or dye it!"

She sounded like a small tiger-cat spitting at him, and almost despite himself the Marquis laughed.

"I apologise, Miss Milford. Go on with what you were telling me."

"I told Giles . . . that is my cousin's name . . . of my predicament . . . and to my delight he told me that he would take me to Paris and leave me at the Convent where I wanted to go."

"And you believed him?"

"I made him swear on everything he held sacred that he would not betray me to Step-Mama. After that he was really obliging about the arrangements."

"So what happened?" the Marquis asked.

"He left yesterday, but instead of going to London, as he told Step-Mama he intended to do, he stayed near our house at a Posting-Inn."

Ola gave a little sigh.

"I had to trust him. There was nobody else who I felt would make an effort to help me."

"What happened?"

"I crept out of the house soon after dawn, and I bribed one of the gardeners, who had always been attached to Papa, to come into the house before the rest of the staff had risen and to collect the trunk I had packed and put ready in my bedroom!"

There was a brief smile on her lips as she said:

"It was easier than I expected, because when I went downstairs to let him in, there was nobody about as I had been half-afraid there might be."

"No night-watchmen, no night-footmen in the Hall?" the Marquis enquired.

"They were all at the other end of the house."

"So you ran away with your luggage," the Marquis said. "What woman would not think of her appearance, even in the most desperate situation?"

"I have already told you," Ola replied, "that I had no money. It would be very silly to spend on clothes what I could obtain by selling my mother's jewellery."

"You have some jewels?"

27

"I suppose it was rather indiscreet of me to mention them, when I intend to travel alone," Ola answered, "but they are all I have between me and starvation!"

"I promise you I will not steal them!"

"I know that," Olga said scornfully. "But I was foolish enough to trust Giles, and now I will never trust a man again . . . never . . . never . . . not even you!"

The Marquis found himself smiling at the anger in her voice. Her eyes, which he now saw in the light from the fire, were green and seemed to have a glint of steel in them.

"I am interested," he said aloud, "to hear what your cousin Giles did that was so reprehensible."

"He helped me to run away. Then halfway to Dover he . . . informed me that he . . . intended to . . . marry me!"

The Marquis laughed.

"That was something you might have anticipated as you are wealthy."

"But Giles is old! He has turned forty, and as he has always been a bachelor, how could I have . . . imagined he would want to . . . marry me?"

She thought that the Marquis was once again going to refer to her money, and she went on:

"Giles said to me: 'I shall be delighted,

when we are married, to administer your fortune, but as I find you unexpectedly attractive, Ola, I shall also enjoy being your husband.' "

"What was your reply to that?" the Marquis asked.

"I told him I would rather die than marry him, and I thought even to suggest such an idea showed that he was a treacherous swine, a Judas whom I should never have trusted in the first place."

"Strong words!" the Marquis said, laughing.

"You may think it funny," Ola cried, "but I knew at that moment I had not only to escape from my Stepmother but . . . also from . . . Giles!"

She drew in her breath before she said:

"There was something about him which . . . frightened me . . . it was not only because he was determined to have my fortune . . . it was the way he looked at me when we stopped for luncheon."

She glanced across the hearth-rug at the Marquis, then continued:

"I expect you think that if I had been clever I would have escaped then, but it was only a small Posting-Inn and there were no other visitors having luncheon except ourselves. If I had tried to run away, Giles could easily have caught me, and it would be difficult to run carrying my jewel-case."

As she spoke she glanced down to where it stood beside her chair.

"I am not criticising," the Marquis said mildly.

"I had originally intended that when I reached here I would take the ordinary cross-Channel ship to France," Ola went on. "But to escape him I must now hire a vessel of some sort."

"Why did he not marry you in England?"

"He had thought of that," Ola answered, "but he was afraid there might be difficulties as he had not my Guardian's permission. He told me he intended to say he was my Guardian, and he thought if he could pay them enough, the French would be more accommodating about performing the marriage-ceremony than an English Parson was likely to be."

"Your cousin had certainly thought things out carefully!" the Marquis remarked.

"Only to his own advantage, and I hate him! It is a pity the accident did not . . . kill him!"

As Ola spoke, the door of the Inn opened and Joe appeared.

"Oi'm sorry, Lady, but Oi finds th' Doctor at Th' Crown and Anchor an' he ain't in no state t' come 'ere tonight. Oi've left a message wi' his mates to tell 'im to be here first thing in th' morn' when he be sobered up."

"Thank you, Joe," Ola replied. "I am very grateful to you."

As she spoke she realised that Joe was waiting for the tip he had been told she had promised him.

She quickly drew a small purse from the inside pocket of her cape, which was still lying behind her on the chair.

Before she could open it, however, the Marquis flicked a gold coin from his side of the fireplace towards Joe, who caught it deftly.

"Thank ye, Sir!" he said with a grin. "Oi'll go upstairs now an' see 'ow th' patient be. The Guv'nor said as 'ow he'd stay with him 'til Oi comes back with th' Doctor."

He disappeared and Ola looked at the Marquis.

"Can we go now . . . at once?" she asked.

"I have not yet said that I will take you with me."

"But you will . . . please . . . say you will! You can leave me at Calais and I will find my own way from there to Paris."

"Alone?"

"There is nobody else to travel with me,

31

unless . . . Giles recovers."

The mere idea made her look up at the ceiling as if she thought to hear the sound of his voice.

"He must not do that . . . he is determined . . . absolutely determined . . . to m-marry me!"

"You could of course tell your story to the Magistrates and ask them to return you to your Stepmother."

"How can you suggest such a thing when I have told you she hates me?" Ola asked. "No . . . I am going to Paris even if I have to buy a boat and row myself across the Channel!"

She gave an exasperated little sigh and added:

"Oh, why does England have to be an island?"

The Marquis smiled.

"It is something that stood us in good stead when Napoleon was trying to invade us!"

"That was a long time ago, and if there was not the sea between us and France, I could ride to Paris or drive there in a *diligence,* although I believe they are very uncomfortable. I saw them often enough when I was at the Convent."

"I cannot imagine either mode of travel

would be particularly enjoyable," the Marquis remarked drily.

"I am not out to enjoy myself," Ola retorted. "You seem not to understand that I am trying to escape from a life of misery, and you must be very insensitive not to understand how much I have suffered."

"I am, as it happens, concerned with my own suffering at the moment," the Marquis commented.

"What can that be? Have you lost a fortune at the gaming-tables? Or been crossed in love? That is not compatible with your reputation, My Lord Marquis!"

She spoke sarcastically, and was surprised by the expression of anger which contorted the Marquis's face.

"You will keep a civil tongue in your head," he said sharply, "or I will leave you here to cope with your problems alone, which in fact I am certain would be the sensible thing for me to do!"

Ola clasped her hands together.

"I am sorry . . . please forgive me . . . it was, I know, very rude . . . and I should not have spoken as I did. Please . . . please . . . help me! If you refuse to do so . . . I think I shall throw myself into the Harbour. I doubt if anyone would notice, and I should just be discovered floating out to sea in the morning!"

She spoke dramatically, and although he was angry the Marquis was forced to laugh. Then he said:

"I accept your apology, but in the future, as you are at my mercy, I suggest you curb your tongue and your imagination, or I shall certainly abandon you to your fate!"

"Please . . . do not do that!"

"If I were wise that is exactly what I should do. It is no affair of mine whom you marry or do not marry, and I have an uneasy suspicion that if I were behaving with a vestige of common sense I should send you back to your Stepmother!"

"But you will not do so," Ola said softly.

"I hate to think what is the alternative."

"I can tell you that," Ola said in a small voice. "It is that you take me to Calais in your . . . yacht. Surely this fog will lift soon?"

As she spoke she rose as if to go towards the door and look out.

At that moment there were heavy footsteps coming down the stairs and a moment later the Proprietor came into the room.

"Oi don't know if ye wish to stay here the night, Ma'am," he said to Ola, "but Oi 'as a small bedroom empty an' could accommodate ye, 'though 'tis not so comfortable as the one th' poor gentleman be in."

Ola looked towards the Marquis.

"I am taking this lady with me," he said, and saw, as he spoke, the expression of delight that transformed Ola's face.

On the other hand, the Proprietor was obviously disappointed.

"What about th' gentleman upstairs?"

"He can look after himself when he gets better," the Marquis replied. "But I understand this lady had a trunk with her in the carriage in which she was travelling. What has happened to it?"

"The servant, who seemed unharmed," the Proprietor replied, "is a-taking th' horses to a stable at th' top of th' road."

"Then send your man Joe to collect the trunk," the Marquis ordered, "and he can follow this lady and me to where my yacht is tied up at the Quay. It is not more than fifty yards from here."

"I'll get him down, Sir," the Proprietor answered.

He went to the bottom of the stairs and started shouting for Joe.

Ola turned towards the Marquis.

"How can I thank you?" she asked. "Thank you . . . thank you! I think you must be an angel sent to save me."

"I think if the truth were told," the Marquis replied, "I am slightly touched in the head, or else the brandy I have imbibed was stronger than I anticipated."

"No, you are a Good Samaritan," Ola said, "for, as I told you, I really have fallen amongst . . . thieves!"

Again as she thought of her cousin upstairs her eyes went towards the ceiling, and the Marquis, seeing the lines of her long neck and the movement of light in her hair, told himself he really was behaving like a fool.

He had sworn when he left home that never again would he have anything to do with women except those who simply sold their favours to the highest bidder.

Never again — and this was a vow he intended to keep for all time — would he be fool enough to imagine himself in love.

Even to think of Sarah made him want to clench his hands and hit something — anything, anybody — to relieve the fury of his feelings.

And yet, despite a lesson which should have made any man hesitate before even looking at or speaking to a woman who called herself a lady, he had quite inadvertently become involved with this girl.

It was simply because it was impossible for him not to feel sorry for her in the predicament in which she found herself.

On the other hand, how did he know

whether what she had told him was the truth? It might be a lie like the lies Sarah had told him.

He felt a sudden impulse to change his mind and tell her that after all she must find her own way out of her difficulties.

Or, easier still, he had only to say he was going outside to see what the weather was like, and then disappear in the fog and never come back.

That would be prudent and sensible, perhaps, but it would also, he thought, be a caddish trick such as he had never lowered himself to play in the past.

But nobleness, chivalry, or sheer decency, call it what you will, had only succeeded in making him the cynic he knew he now was and would be for the rest of his life.

"Never trust a woman — they always betray you!"

It sounded like a quotation he must have heard somewhere, unless it was a conviction that came from the depths of his heart.

The mere thought of Sarah made him feel as if his body were on fire, while his anger swept over him and there was a red film in front of his eyes.

He wanted to curse her aloud, and he wished now that he had given himself the satisfaction of telling her plainly what he thought of her before he had walked away, determined never to see her again.

'Dammit all — I am running away!' he had thought as he drove towards Dover.

But something sensitive and vulnerable within him shrank from the scene which would have followed had he told Sarah what he had discovered and seen with his own eyes.

She could have lied, she would have pleaded with him, and if she had finally suffered defeat and found that she could not again cajole him into wishing to marry her, she might have laughed at him!

That was something he knew he could not endure simply because he deserved it.

For the first time in his life, in his very successful career as both a sportsman and a lover, the Marquis, the most acclaimed and envied man in Society, had been "hoist by his own petard."

Even now, a whole day after it had happened, he found it hard to believe it was true.

He had become used to being a conqueror; he had grown used to knowing, although he told himself he was not conceited about it, that any woman he fancied was only too ready to fall into his arms.

Most of all, there was no woman in the

length and breadth of the Kingdom who would not jump at the chance of becoming his wife.

As soon as he looked at them he would see the excitement in their eyes and it told him exactly what they longed for and undoubtedly prayed for.

"We will be married, my darling," he could hear himself say to Sarah, "as soon as you are out of mourning. I cannot wait a day longer than I have to."

"Oh, Boyden!" Sarah had cried. "I love you, and I swear I will make you happy, just as you have already made me the happiest woman in the world!"

Her voice was very soft and seductive as she said the last words, and as her blue eyes looked up into his, the Marquis had believed that he had found the pearl beyond price which he had always sought in the woman he would marry.

Then yesterday evening everything he had planned, his whole future, had fallen in pieces about his ears.

CHAPTER TWO

The Marquis awoke when he heard the anchor being raised and a few minutes later the yacht began to heel over as the sails were set and caught the wind.

He was aware that his head ached and his mouth felt dry, and he knew that last night, contrary to his usual habit, he had drunk too much.

First, the brandy had been surprisingly good at the Inn on the Quay, and secondly, when he had returned to the yacht he felt so depressed and incensed with life in general that he had sent the steward for a decanter of his best claret, which he had drunk until the early hours of the morning.

Then, when he thought of last night, he remembered that he had brought a woman aboard with him, and he asked himself if he had gone insane.

How, after all that happened, after an experience that should have been the lesson of a lifetime, could he have been mad enough to involve himself with yet another woman and one who, if he was not careful, would undoubtedly be an encumbrance?

Then, because it was impossible for his thoughts to linger for long on anything except the perfidy of Sarah, he recalled the reason why he was in Dover, why he had drunk too much, and why in the cold and unpleasantness of March he should be contemplating a voyage at sea.

Thinking back, he could remember all too clearly the moment when he had met Sarah.

He had been so occupied in London that he had not been down to Elvin last winter as much as usual.

He had been involved in many discussions and committees concerning the projected Reform Bill and in speaking frequently on other matters in the Chamber of the House of Lords.

He had also found that the new King, William IV, required his presence constantly at Buckingham Palace.

While it was flattering to be in such demand, it meant that he seldom had any free time for his own amusement.

It had therefore been almost with a feeling of playing truant that he had slipped away from London to Elvin, to enjoy a few days' hunting before the season ended.

He was well in the front of the field and enjoying one of the best runs he had experienced for a long time when, crossing some rough ground, his horse picked up a stone.

As he was riding one of his very best hunters, the Marquis dismounted, and, letting the hunt go on without him, he realised that he must either try to dislodge the stone himself or find someone to do it for him.

He had, as it happened, nothing he could use as a probe except for his fingers, and when he lifted his horse's hoof he saw that the stone was embedded half under the shoe and if it was not extracted carefully the shoe would come away with it.

He looked round and saw that he was on his own Estate, which was a very extensive one, and that only a short distance from where he was standing was the Manor.

He remembered his Agent telling him a year ago that it had been let to Sir Robert Chesney.

Ordinarily the Marquis would have called on a new tenant, but he had in fact forgotten Sir Robert's arrival, and when he had come to Elvin it had been with large parties and he had no time to pay courtesy calls on local people.

"I shall have to make my apologies now," he told himself as, leading his horse by the bridle, he walked towards the Manor.

He went immediately to the stables and found an elderly groom to whom he explained his predicament.

The groom recognised him and, touching his forelock, said:

"Now don' ee worry, M'Lord. Oi'll soon get th' stone away, then ye can rejoin th' hunt. Oi can 'ear 'em now, drawing through Chandle's Wood, but Oi doubts they'll find anything there!"

"I imagine that is where the fox has gone to earth," the Marquis replied.

"If 'e 'as, then they'll 'ave to dig deep!" the groom said with a smile.

He took the horse as he spoke and led it towards an empty stall.

"While you are busy," the Marquis said, "I will pay my respects to Sir Robert. He is at home?"

The groom's voice altered as he answered:

"Sir Robert died last week, M'Lord!"

"I had no idea!" the Marquis exclaimed.

He thought as he spoke that it was extremely remiss of his Agent not to have informed him of the fact.

It would have been polite to send Sir Robert's widow a letter of condolence or at least to send a wreath to the Funeral.

"Oi be sure 'er Ladyship'd wish to make yer acquaintance, M'Lord," the groom said.

The Marquis walked towards the front door, feeling uncomfortably that he owed

Lady Chesney an apology.

An elderly man-servant led him across the small Hall and into what the Marquis remembered was a charming Drawing-Room which overlooked the rose-garden at the back of the house.

If he thought the room was charming, then so was its occupant.

She was certainly astonished to see him when he was announced, but he liked the manner in which her voice when she greeted him was calm and composed, and he certainly liked her appearance.

In a black gown which accentuated her clear skin, the gold of her hair, and the blue of her eyes, Lady Chesney was certainly very alluring.

She insisted on sending for some refreshment, and as the Marquis seated himself opposite her he said:

"I have only just learnt from your groom of your husband's death. I can only say how sorry I am not to have sent you my condolences and my sympathy, but now they are both yours."

"That is very kind of you, My Lord," Lady Chesney answered. "My husband had been ill for some years, and the reason why we came here was that the Physicians thought the fresh air and the quiet of the country might do him good."

She paused before she said with a little sob:

"Unfortunately they were . . . mistaken."

That was the beginning of an acquaintance that progressed rapidly into friendship, and from friendship into love.

The Marquis, riding away from the Manor, found it impossible to forget the blue eyes which had looked at him pathetically, curiously, and then undoubtedly admiringly.

He had returned the next day, feeling that since he had not sent a wreath to the Funeral, he could at least provide the widow with exotic fruit and flowers from his greenhouses.

She had been suitably grateful and of course had said how interested she would be to see Elvin, as she had always heard so much about it.

The Marquis was only too willing to be her guide, and her delight at the treasures that had been accumulated by his ancestors and at the innovations he himself had made in the house was very gratifying.

It was six months before the Marquis became what he had wished to be within a week or so after making her acquaintance — Sarah Chesney's lover.

But he had found that to accomplish this required all his powers of persuasion and ingenuity.

This was not because she did not love him.

She had told him that she had loved him at first sight and that he had captured her heart to the point where it was no longer hers but his.

However, she was anxious that there should be no breath of scandal, which, she had said, might so easily spoil the love they had for each other.

She had explained it in a way which the Marquis thought was good common sense.

"You are so fascinating and so handsome, My Lord," she had said, "that naturally every woman you meet falls in love with you. The world being a censorious place, no-one would believe that any one female could resist your magical charm."

"You flatter me!" the Marquis had said with a smile, but he had enjoyed it all the same.

"You will understand," Sarah had gone on in a soft, caressing voice, "that I could not be disloyal to my dear Robert's memory by getting myself talked about in a scandalous manner so soon after his death. While you can go back to London and forget me, I have to live in this small world in which people talk because they have nothing better to do."

"Do you really think I could forget you?" the Marquis asked.

"I hope you will not do so," Sarah replied. "But you are so important and of such consequence in the Social World, while I am just a little nobody who worships you because you have brought me such unbelievable happiness."

"You know that happiness is what I want to bring you," the Marquis said, "and I want to show you how much I love you. But as you say, it is impossible here at the Manor, where your servants might be suspicious of what we were doing."

"They are so kind to me," Sarah said. "They look after me and cosset me. But they would be deeply shocked if they thought you were anything more than a kind friend who wished to comfort me in my loneliness."

The situation had seemed hopeless until Sarah was asked to stay with some friends on the other side of the County with whom the Marquis had a slight acquaintance.

It had not been easy, but because he was determined he had somehow managed to get himself invited at the same time.

They pretended that they had never met before. Fortunately there were quite a number of other people staying in the house and their bedrooms were not far apart.

The Marquis, making love to a woman he had pursued for six months, found it a delight that made him feel as if he had won a victory after what had been a strenuous battle.

He believed too that he was in love with Sarah as he had never been in love before.

The only difficulty was how they could contrive to continue their love-making, which the Marquis was certain had been as unforgettable an experience for her as it had been for him.

There had been another month of frustration during which, despite his pleadings, Sarah had refused to agree to what he asked of her and had made him feel he was a brute to suggest anything that might damage her reputation.

"If I cannot come to your house and you will not come to mine," he asked, "what are we to do about each other?"

Her eyes filled with tears as they looked into his and she said in a broken little voice:

"Oh, Boyden, I love you so desperately! But . . ."

'There is always that "but"!' the Marquis

later thought irritably.

Then it suddenly struck him that the answer to their problem was quite obvious. He would marry Sarah!

He had always known that sooner or later he must marry and produce an heir, but it had not seemed a pressing necessity until he was over thirty, which would not be for another year.

What was more, he enjoyed being a bachelor and had seen far too many of his friends unhappily married to women who had seemed desirable enough until they actually bore their husbands' names and sat at the top of their tables.

"Marriage is hell, Elvington!" Lord Wickham had said to him after being married for only three months.

"But Charlotte is so beautiful," the Marquis had replied.

"That is what I thought, until I saw her in the mornings when she is petulant, and in the evenings when she is tired. And I will tell you another thing," Lord Wickham had gone on, "it is not the looks of a wife that count, it is her intelligence."

His lips tightened for a moment before he had continued:

"Can you imagine what it is like to know exactly what a woman is going to say before she says it, for twenty-four hours of the day?"

The Marquis had not replied, and his friend had said bitterly:

"You are the only one of our crowd who has had the sense to remain a bachelor. George's wife takes laudanum, and Charles has married a harridan!"

"I have certainly no wish to be leg-shackled!" the Marquis said firmly not only to his friends but to himself.

And yet, he thought, Sarah was different, so different and so ideal in every way, so exactly what a man wanted in his wife, that he dared not risk losing her.

He knew even then that he hesitated before committing himself.

In fact, he was now considering Sarah from a somewhat different angle. She was not only a very desirable woman who set his pulses racing and his heart throbbing when she was near, she was someone he could trust.

She would also, he thought, be able to take his mother's place as hostess in the houses he owned and, more important still, be as acceptable at Buckingham Palace as he was himself.

He knew this involved something very different from what it would have meant under the last Monarch.

George IV up until his dying day had liked the men who surrounded him to be raffish and witty and, because it was what he himself had always been, promiscuous as regards women.

What was more, the ladies who were admitted to the Royal Circle were expected to be attractive to the opposite sex and not to be too particular or difficult as regards their morals.

But Buckingham Palace today had a very different atmosphere. The Marquis often thought it was not the same place now that the staid and prudish little Queen Adelaide was on the throne.

There was no doubt that she and her much older husband were extremely happy together, but while the King had enjoyed a riotous youth and had fathered ten illegitimate children by the actress Mrs. Jordan, he had now become so respectable that, as one Statesman had remarked to the Marquis:

"I always feel as I enter the Palace that I am attending a Prayer-Meeting!"

The Marquis had laughed, but he knew that if he wished to keep his place at Court, his life must be circumspect in every way.

If there was the slightest breath of scandal about his wife, Queen Adelaide would make sure that she was excluded from the Royal Circle.

Watching Sarah critically, the Marquis became more convinced every time he saw her that she would make exactly the wife he required.

Although he had to control his desires, which he found both irritating and frustrating, he still admired her for sticking to her principles and making him understand mentally, if not physically, that they were really necessary.

Only when finally he had proposed marriage, and she had said in a rapturous manner that her dreams and her ambitions had been fulfilled, did she relent a little and, as he put it to himself, "lower the drawbridge."

"I love you! How can I wait months before you can be mine?" the Marquis had asked.

"I want you too," Sarah had whispered, "and so, my darling, I have an idea!"

"What is it?"

"My lady's-maid, who I always feel watches me like a hawk, has left today to visit her mother, who is ill. That means there is only an old couple in the house, both of whom are deaf."

"You mean . . . ?" the Marquis had asked, his eyes brightening as he realised what she was saying.

"If you come to me tonight, dearest, nobody will know that you are here and I can be in your arms as I long to be."

The Marquis had kissed her until they were both breathless, then Sarah had said:

"Come to me across the garden. You can leave your horse tied to a tree in the shrubbery and I will open the French window after the servants have gone to bed."

"My sweet! My darling!" the Marquis had cried.

When later he had said a formal farewell in front of the old Butler, their eyes met and he knew that they were both counting the hours until they could be together again.

They had spent two nights of bliss. Then Sarah told him that her maid had returned, and because the Marquis could not bear to toss restlessly in his bed at Elvin, when he longed to be with Sarah in hers, he had gone back to London.

There was a great deal for him to do, and, because he was genuinely interested in politics, the difficulties of the Reform Bill fully occupied his mind during the days.

But at night he found it impossible to sleep, and like a boy at School he crossed the days off on his calendar until Sarah's official mourning would be over and they could be married.

She would be free on March third but they agreed that it would be politic to wait another month. To the Marquis the thought was like a light glowing in the darkness.

He had already bought Sarah an engagement-ring and several expensive jewels to go with it.

They were locked in a drawer of his desk, waiting for the moment when he could give them to her and the world could be told that she was to be his wife.

Then his longing to see her again made him know that he must go back to Elvin. Even if he could not make love to her as he wanted to do, he could at least hold her in his arms, kiss her, and hear her pay him compliments in her soft, musical voice.

He was wondering when he should go to her, when he received a letter and at the mere sight of her handwriting he felt his heart turn over.

"I have never been so much in love as I am now!" he told himself.

He opened the letter and read:

Hannah, my maid, has been told today that her mother has died. She is therefore leaving immediately for the Funeral, and you know, dearest, wonderful Boyden, this means we can be together as we both long to be.

I know that you will be counting the hours, as I am, until we can touch the wings of ecstasy!

Come to me in the usual way across the garden tomorrow, at half-after-nine-o'clock. The servants go to bed early, and I shall be waiting for you . . . waiting . . . waiting until I feel your arms round me.

I love you!
Sarah

The Marquis read and reread the note and told himself that no woman could be so loving, so adorable, and so exactly right in every way to be the Marchioness of Elvington.

"I am the most fortunate man in the world," he said aloud, "and I shall see her tomorrow!"

Then he read the letter again.

She had said that her maid Hannah was leaving today. In which case, why wait until tomorrow and miss being together tonight?

He looked at the clock.

He had risen early and the letter had been waiting on his breakfast-table.

He calculated that if he left London within the next hour he could be at Elvington about eight o'clock.

After he had dined he would ride across

the Park and through the fields as he had done before and be at the Manor by about ten o'clock.

The window would not be open for him but the servants would be in bed, and if Sarah was in her bedroom he could easily attract her attention from the garden without disturbing anybody else in the house.

"I will surprise her!" he told himself with a smile, thinking of her delight and what an excitement his arrival would be to both of them because it was unexpected.

He gave the order for his Phaeton and his fastest team of four horses to be brought round immediately, and soon he was on his way to Elvin.

His arrival was no surprise to his servants because his staff had instructions always to be ready to receive him and his Chef prepared to produce a superb menu without having any previous notice of his arrival.

The Marquis, having bathed and changed, ate an excellent dinner, waited on by his Butler and three footmen. At precisely nine-forty-five he went to the front door to find one of his fastest horses waiting outside.

Because he often rode at night after dinner, he thought his staff would not have the least suspicion as to where he was going. He would therefore have been extremely annoyed if he had known that everyone in the house, from the Butler to the youngest knife-boy, was aware of his infatuation for the widow who lived at the Manor.

"All I can say," one of the footmen said to another as he rode away, "is that she's been lucky to catch His Lordship. There's not a gentleman to equal him in the sportin' world."

"You're right there," his companion replied, "and I suppose she'll suit him all right. But I'd never fancy a widow meself."

"Why not?" his friend enquired.

"I likes to be first!" was the answer. "First past the winning-post and first in bed!"

There was laughter at this, and it was fortunate that the Marquis, crossing the Park in front of the house, was unaware that his staff did not suppose he was just enjoying the evening air.

Once out of sight of the house, he galloped because he was in a hurry to reach Sarah.

He thought romantically that the noise of the horse's hoofs repeated over and over again the three words that were uppermost in his mind:

"I love you! I love you! I love you!"

At the end of the Park he passed through a wood, then over several fields, until at last he could see ahead of him the shrubbery which bordered the garden of the Manor.

He knew exactly where he could tether his horse, and having done so he walked surely and without hesitating along the twisting path which skirted the rhododendrons and ended at the edge of the rose-garden, in the centre of which was a sun-dial.

It was then that he was aware that the lights were on not only in Sarah's bedroom but also in the Drawing-Room.

The Marquis stood still.

It suddenly occurred to him that perhaps Sarah was entertaining, which would explain why she had asked him to come tomorrow instead of tonight.

Then he told himself that she would never have expected anyway that he would have received her letter so early and have left London immediately.

She knew how meticulously he always planned his various engagements, and in fact he had done something unprecedented for him when this morning he had sent messages to no fewer than four people to offer his regrets that he could not keep the appointments he had made with them.

"When I tell her, she will appreciate how much I love her," the Marquis told himself.

But now, looking across the darkness of the garden towards the light, he was uncertain.

The last thing he should do was to walk in unexpectedly if Sarah was entertaining their neighbours.

Then it struck him that despite the fact that there were lights in the Drawing-Room, everything seemed very quiet.

Although he was listening intently, he could hear no chatter of voices or laughter as might have been expected.

"Perhaps she has not yet gone to bed," he told himself. "She may be sitting reading or sewing in the Drawing-Room and if I knock on the window she will open it."

He took a step forward from the shelter of the rhododendrons and as he did so he saw the long French window open, and someone was standing against the light.

'She is waiting for me,' he thought.

They were so attuned to each other, he told himself, that she had known perceptively, almost clairvoyantly, that he was coming and had opened the window to welcome him in.

There was a rapturous smile on the Marquis's lips as he took another step forward.

Then suddenly he saw that Sarah was not alone.

A man had appeared beside her and hastily the Marquis retreated into the shadows.

Now he saw Sarah turn her face up towards the man beside her, and the next moment she was in his arms and he was kissing her!

At first the Marquis could hardly believe that what he was seeing was not a figment of his imagination or a part of some terrible nightmare.

Then the moon came out from behind the clouds and he could see more clearly than he had before.

Sarah was wearing her blue negligé. He knew it well, and when he had last seen it she had been letting him out of the window, as she was doing now with the man she was kissing.

What was more, the Marquis recognised who he was.

He was the handsome younger son of a Peer whom the Marquis had found, since he had inherited Elvin, a considerable nuisance.

Because the boundaries of their two Estates marched together, Lord Harrop was always sending complaints of one sort or another to the Marquis.

He knew that the reason for most of them was that Lord Harrop was far from wealthy and was determined to extort from his rich neighbour every concession and help for his own Estate that was possible.

The Marquis was well aware that Lord Harrop's sons — and there were four of them — were jealous of the horses he rode at the local Point-to-Points and at the Steeple-Chases which he invariably won.

It was not his fault, but it flashed through his mind now that Anthony had his revenge in taking from him the only woman he had ever wished to marry.

Then as he watched Anthony kiss Sarah before he stepped out through the window and onto the terrace outside, the Marquis felt the blood rush to his head.

He wanted to fight Anthony, to knock him down and even to kill him.

Then, not only years of self-control kept him from moving, but a pride which told him that he had been made a fool of not only by Sarah but by a man younger than himself whom he had always thought too insignificant even to consider as a rival.

As the Marquis battled with himself, he realised that Anthony was walking towards him and in the space of a few seconds they would meet face to face.

He clenched his fists together.

Then as he was not quite certain what he would do, he heard Sarah's voice, soft and sweet as it had so often been to him, call out:

"Anthony, darling, I have something more to say to you."

His rival turned back and it was then that the Marquis knew he must escape.

He retreated, moving swiftly back the way he had come, and found his horse.

It was only as he mounted that he saw Anthony's horse about fifty yards farther along the side of the shrubbery.

In the darkness before the moon came out he had not noticed it, but now he could see it quite clearly.

The Marquis wasted no time, he just rode away, hoping that Anthony would not see him go.

It was only when he reached home and walked upstairs to his own room that he felt numb with shock, and there was at the same time a growing anger deep within him that seemed to increase as every minute passed.

He allowed his valet to help him undress but he did not speak, and only when he was alone did the Marquis ask himself what he should do.

He knew he could not stay in England to

face Sarah and the explanations that would have to be made and the scene that would follow.

He knew too, because he was deeply humiliated by what he had seen, that it would take him some time to control himself to the point where he could appear indifferent.

At the moment he was angry and hurt, wounded and jealous, murderous and yet at the same time weak, with a kind of misery that he knew would increase because he had lost something which he had thought was more valuable than anything he had ever possessed before.

He asked himself a thousand times how he could have been so foolish as to be deceived like any greenhorn by what he knew now was a scheming woman.

He had no doubt that Sarah had intended to marry him from the first moment they had met.

He could see all too clearly that by playing "hard to get" she had excited and enticed him into offering her exactly what she wanted, which was marriage.

The Marquis admitted frankly that usually his love-affairs did not last very long.

Once a woman had surrendered herself, he found that the repetition of their love-making soon became tedious and he began to wonder what it would be like to pursue another beauty and whether she would be more original or more captivating than the one he was with now.

Sarah had been too clever to allow him to feel like that, and had driven him crazy by bestowing her favours after a long wooing and then withholding them again.

The Marquis gritted his teeth when he thought of how he had fallen into the trap that women have set for men ever since the days of Adam and Eve.

Each move had been traditional, almost like a game of chess, but he had not had the intelligence to see it until now.

Then he told himself in the darkness of the night that he could not face Sarah because all he could really accuse her of was being more astute than he was.

'I have to get away,' he thought, and remembered that his yacht was waiting ready for him at Dover.

It was three months since he had last used it, and then only for a short journey across the Channel with a friend who wished to fight a duel without anyone in England being aware of it.

He knew that on his orders the yacht was always ready to put to sea at a moment's notice.

He had risen before dawn and left Elvin when the stars were still shining in the sky.

The Marquis could hear the slap of the sea against the bow of the yacht as they were under way, and as the timbers creaked and there was the rasp in the rigging, he felt the sails fill and knew there was a strong wind blowing.

"At least there will be nothing to hold us up," he told himself.

He had given his Captain instructions the night before, and it should take them less than five hours to reach Calais, where he would deposit his passenger. After that, he would be free to sail anywhere in the world that took his fancy.

He wondered now if Ola would manage on the way to Paris, then told himself that it was none of his business.

It must have been the brandy last night that had made him feel he ought to help her out of what must have been for her a frightening situation — that is, if he was to believe what she had told him.

There was no doubt that the man who had been involved in the accident through driving his horses in a pea-soup fog was elderly, and the girl with her flaming red hair was very young.

But perhaps she was deceitful and a liar, the Marquis thought scornfully, as all women were — damn them!

"When I return to England there will be no more 'Sarahs' in my life," he said aloud, "and no more games of pretence."

He could almost hear himself saying the loving words to Sarah which now made him blush with embarrassment.

Although he had thought she genuinely meant the sentimental promises which lovers make to each other, all the time she had been laughing at him.

Doubtless too she held him up to ridicule with the man she really loved, penniless Anthony, who had been her lover those nights when, alone at Elvin, he had felt frustrated and solitary because Sarah was worrying about her "reputation."

"Her reputation!"

The Marquis laughed bitterly.

These were the words he had repeated to himself when he drove his superb horses from Elvin to where the road joined the main highway to Dover.

At the first Coaching-Inn he changed his horses for those that were kept for him month after month, just in case he should need them.

There was another change later on, and

these horses should have brought him easily to Dover before dusk.

But then they had run into the fog, and it was only by superb driving and because the Marquis knew the way so well that he had managed to board his yacht and inform the Captain that he wished to put to sea immediately.

"I regret, M'Lord, that's completely impossible!" the Captain had replied.

"You mean because of the fog?"

"No ship could move in this weather, M'Lord. There's not enough wind to fill a pocket-handkerchief!"

"Then we will leave as soon as it is possible."

"Where to, M'Lord?"

This was something the Marquis had not considered and he said after a moment:

"I will tell you later."

"Very good, M'Lord. I hope we have everything Your Lordship'll need aboard. We took on fresh water and supplies yesterday."

The Marquis nodded, but he was not interested in the details of his yacht-equipment. It was just a vehicle, almost a Magic Carpet, to carry him away not only from England but from Sarah.

When he dined he could not bear to be alone with his thoughts, and he walked through the fog to where he saw the lights of The Three Bells.

Now he wished he had made use of the fog to escape from yet another woman.

He had the uncomfortable feeling that he had made a fundamental mistake in agreeing to carry that redhead — what was her name? — Ola, to France.

If her Stepmother caught up with her and learnt that she had been assisted by the Marquis of Elvington, all sorts of constructions might be put on what had been a simple act of charity.

"I have been a fool once again!" the Marquis told himself. "What the hell is the matter with me? Of course I should have left her at the Inn."

Instead of being, as she had said, a Good Samaritan, he could easily find himself accused of being interested in the girl personally, and if her Guardian was anything near as ambitious as Sarah, he might be expected to make reparation by offering her marriage.

"I am damned if I will do that!" the Marquis said angrily.

Then he told himself that he was being needlessly apprehensive. He would do what the girl had asked, would drop her at Calais, and then would forget about her.

By the time she had got herself into trouble he could easily be on the other side of the world, but where he intended to go he had not yet decided.

'I suppose the Mediterranean would be best, at any rate as a start,' he thought.

He remembered that Smollet had eulogised over Nice and he knew that the climate would be springlike at the moment and there would be sunshine and a blue sea.

"It might as well be Nice as anywhere else," he told himself.

The sea would be blue! That made him think of Sarah's eyes.

"She is haunting me — that is what she is doing!" he exclaimed.

Then he thought of how she had put her arms round Anthony's neck and lifted her face in a way that was very familiar and which he confidently believed was the way she greeted only him.

Had she not said again and again that she loved him as she had never loved anybody else?

There was a red blaze of anger before his eyes and once again he found himself clenching his fists.

"Damn her! Damn her! Damn her!" he said aloud, and the sound of his voice mingled with the whistle of the wind and the sudden slap of the sails as the ship listed to starboard.

"We are in for a rough passage," the Marquis told himself.

CHAPTER THREE

Ola was so tired that, unlike the Marquis, she did not hear the anchor being raised or know that the ship was pitching and tossing as soon as they were out of Harbour.

Instead she slept deeply and dreamlessly until a knock on the door awakened her.

When she said: "Come in!" a steward appeared, moving unsteadily across the cabin to put a closed cup, such as she had heard was used at sea in rough weather, down beside her bed.

"We're in for a rough passage, Miss," he said. "I've brought you some coffee, and if you'd like something more substantial the Chef'll do his best, but it's a bit difficult to work in the galley at the moment."

"Coffee is all I want," Ola replied, "and thank you very much."

"I should stay where you are, Miss, if you'll take my advice," the steward said before he left. "It's easy for 'land-lubbers,' as we calls 'em, to break a leg when the weather's so bad."

Ola knew that he was being tactful in not suggesting she might be sea-sick, but as it happened she was aware that she was a good sailor.

Her father had been very fond of the sea and when she was a small child he had often taken her out in a boat and she had soon learnt that however rough it might be, she was unaffected.

When the steward had gone, she thought that she should have asked him at what time they would reach Calais.

She had the feeling that if she was not ready to go ashore as soon as they docked, it would irritate the Marquis.

When they had walked to the ship last night in the thick fog she had known, although he had said nothing, that he was annoyed by his own generosity in offering to take her across the Channel.

He had abruptly instructed a steward to show her to a cabin, and she had told herself that it had really been "touch and go" as to whether he fulfilled his role of being a Good Samaritan or abandoned her to her fate.

She shuddered now as she thought of how horrible it would have been to have to marry Giles. She had never really thought of him as a man until the moment when he had revealed his treachery because he desired her fortune.

'It is a great mistake to have so much

money,' she thought to herself, 'and if Papa had had a son I would not now be in this predicament.'

At the same time, son or no son, she knew that her father had not been able to escape from her Stepmother once she had made up her mind to marry him.

Ola could understand only too well how easily it had happened.

She had been at the Convent in France when her mother died.

There had been no chance of her getting back in time for the Funeral, and her father had therefore not sent for her or even told her by letter what had occurred, but instead had come himself to break the news to her gently.

They had cried together for the woman they had both loved. Then her father had returned to England alone, and that, Ola had told herself over and over again, had been a fatal mistake.

Of course she should have gone with him to look after him, but it had never occurred to either of them that she should cease her education because of her father's bereavement.

It was only when she was seventeen and had completed the two years she was to spend in France, as had been arranged by her mother, that she returned to England, to find that she was too late.

Her father had been lonely, miserable, and without anyone near him to whom he could talk about his beloved wife.

Her Stepmother, who was a neighbour, had, with the charm and sweetness that she could switch on so easily when it suited her, wormed her way into his confidence until he felt she was indispensable to him.

They were married just two days before Ola arrived home, and she knew as soon as she met her Stepmother that the haste was deliberate so that she could not interfere.

She saw that her Stepmother, all too obviously, wanted more than anything else the social position of being Lady Milford and to be married to a man who could provide her with the money she had always craved.

The face she showed him was a very different one from what his daughter saw.

Ola supposed that she must have met her father's new wife in the past, but she could not remember when, and it was doubtful that Lady Milford would have paid much attention to the young daughter of a neighbour whom she did not often see.

But a child in the Nursery or in the School-Room was very different from a stepdaughter with a spectacular beauty, and when Lord Milford died, Ola inherited a large fortune that exceeded by a dozen times what had been left to his widow.

Lady Milford had from the first been jealous of Ola, but now she was also envious of her money, and her hatred exploded almost like an anarchist's bomb.

Ola had only very briefly described to the Marquis what she had suffered. It would have been impossible to tell him of the agony she had endured in what was a continuous mental persecution, besides being afraid of her Stepmother physically.

Because she knew that Lady Milford disliked her good looks to the point where even to see her aroused her anger, Ola had always been nervous that she would find some way of damaging her face, as sometimes in a temper she threatened to do.

Then, because she had both spirit and courage, Ola was determined to escape.

She was well aware that it was not going to be easy, but as she became more and more a prisoner in the home where she had once been so happy, she knew that somehow, however difficult it might be, she must get away.

Giles had proved to be an undoubted Judas when she had least expected it, and that had been a blow which might have made somebody with less character collapse completely.

Then like a miracle, Ola thought, she had found the Marquis, and now in his yacht she was safe for the moment, whatever difficulties lay ahead.

When she had drunk the coffee, being careful not to spill any of it on the fine linen sheets which were embroidered with the Marquis's monogram, she lay back against the pillows and tried to think.

She had spoken to the Marquis of the *diligences* but she remembered that they were slow and used by all sorts and conditions of people, some of whom might be very rough.

The most sensible thing, she thought, would be to take a post-chaise to Paris.

But it would be expensive and she would not have enough money to pay for one without selling some of her jewellery.

'I must talk to the Marquis about that,' she thought.

Then something fastidious made her feel that it was embarrassing to discuss money with the man who had befriended her against his will and would be wishing to be rid of her as soon as possible.

"There must be a good jeweller in Calais," she told herself. "I will ask what he will pay me for one of Mama's smaller diamond brooches. When I get to the Convent I will give the rest of the jewels to the Mother-Superior to keep safely until I require some more money."

Then a sudden thought struck her and she opened her eyes to stare unseeingly, but with a definite expression of desperate anxiety, across the small cabin.

It was after midday when the Marquis came down from the deck to where his valet was waiting for him at the bottom of the companionway to help him out of his oil-skin coat.

"Your Lordship's not wet, I hopes?" he asked solicitously.

"No, Gibson," the Marquis replied. "And it is an exhilarating experience to see how fast the *Sea Wolf* moves with the wind behind her."

"It is indeed, M'Lord," Gibson replied. "I always said Your Lordship was right in choosing this type of ship for what you requires."

"I am always right, Gibson!" the Marquis said half-jokingly, but with an inner conviction that told him it was in fact the truth.

There had been a battle to get the ship-builders to design a yacht on the exact lines that he required. But he had seen when he was a boy the performance of the Naval Frigates in the war, and he had sworn that if he was ever in the position of building a yacht of his own, he would build one on those lines.

When he was older he had made it his job to examine and sail in the fast Schooners to which the name "Clipper" was first attached.

Their hull design was to become a model for the famous square-rigged Clippers that were being built in the American ship-yards and were only slowly being adopted by the English.

What the Marquis finally evolved for himself was a Schooner with the swiftness of a Frigate but which fortunately did not require such a large crew.

When the *Sea Wolf* was finally launched it caused a sensation amongst sea-faring enthusiasts and the Marquis was congratulated not only by his friends but a great many Naval authorities.

This was the first time, however, that he had taken the *Sea Wolf* out in such a tempestuous sea.

Watching her this morning riding the waves in a manner which he could not fault, he had known that all his ideas which had been called revolutionary had been proved right.

Walking carefully but with the sureness of a man who is used to the sea, the Marquis went into the Saloon, saying as he did so:

"Tell the stewards I am ready for a good meal. I am hungry!"

Then as he finished speaking he saw that he was not alone.

In the comfortable Saloon, where he had designed all the furnishings himself, there was the woman whose very existence he had forgotten for the last two hours.

"Good-morning, My Lord," Ola said. "Forgive me for not rising to greet you, but I feel it would be rather difficult to curtsey when the ship is rolling at this angle."

"Good-morning — Ola!" the Marquis replied.

There was a pause before he said her name because it took him a moment to remember it.

He sat down in a chair not far from her before he asked:

"You are feeling all right? You are not sea-sick?"

"Not in the least," Ola replied, "and if you will allow me to do so, I would like to come up on deck after luncheon. I have never been in a ship that can travel as fast as this one."

"Are you telling me you enjoy the sea?"

"I love it!" Ola replied simply.

"I am glad to hear that," the Marquis said, "because I have some bad news for you."

Ola looked at him enquiringly and he said:

"Last night I ordered my Captain to make for Calais, but so strong a gale has blown up from the Northeast that we cannot make the coast of France. All we can do is run before it out into the English Channel."

As the Marquis spoke he had not really thought of what Ola's reaction would be.

Now as he saw her green eyes light up and a smile appear on her lips, he told himself he might have anticipated that she would prove an unwanted guest who had no wish to relieve herself of his hospitality.

As if she knew what he was thinking, Ola said:

"You are so kind, My Lord, in saying you would take me to France that you must not be . . . annoyed when I say I am . . . delighted to know that I do not have to . . . leave this lovely yacht as . . . quickly as I had . . . anticipated."

The Marquis was not quite certain how it happened, but as the steward brought them a meal he found himself telling Ola about his yacht and the difficulties he had had in having it built in accordance with his ideas.

"I had to fight every inch of the way, or

rather every inch of the ship!" he said. "And only when it was finally finished did the ship-builders stop croaking that my design was impracticable, unworkable, and that she would sink or turn turtle at the first rough sea we encountered."

"I am glad she is doing neither at the moment," Ola said with a laugh.

"You are quite safe," the Marquis said. "She is the most sea-worthy ship afloat, and I am prepared to stake my fortune and my reputation on it!"

They talked of ships and of the *Sea Wolf* in particular the whole time they were at luncheon, and it was only when they had finished that the Marquis said:

"When the wind drops and we can make our way to the French coast, I have been thinking that if we overshoot Le Havre, which is likely, then I may have to take you as far as Bordeaux."

"Are you sailing through the Bay of Biscay?" Ola enquired.

"I am going to the Mediterranean," the Marquis replied, "and there I thought I would put into Nice."

He spoke almost as if he were talking to himself, then as he saw the expression on Ola's face he realised that he had made a mistake.

He had no intention in any circumstances of keeping her aboard one minute after it was possible to put her ashore.

"Bordeaux would suit me very well, My Lord," she said, "if it is not possible to make . . . Le Havre."

Her reply, the Marquis told himself, was one thing, but the hope he saw in her eyes was another.

'I should never have brought her in the first place,' he thought.

He remembered Sarah and the way she had cajoled him into doing what he did not wish to do, and his hatred of women, every one of them, swept over him.

"I can assure you that my Captain is doing his best to reach Le Havre," he said sharply, "and it would be a mistake for you to come on deck. It is extremely cold and you would get wet."

He rose from his seat as he spoke, and without looking at Ola he went from the Saloon.

She gave a little sigh.

She knew it would only make him angry if she argued.

"I wonder what has upset him," she pondered, and was quite certain in her own mind that it was a woman.

Because the Marquis was so good-looking

and undoubtedly very rich, it seemed un-likely, if not impossible, that any woman he fancied would not throw herself into his arms if that was what he wanted.

Yet perhaps, like everybody else, he wanted the unattainable, although what that might be Ola could not imagine.

If she was not allowed to go on deck, she thought, at least there were a number of books in a bookcase on one side of the Saloon.

It had surprised her that there were books aboard the yacht, for she knew that when her father was at sea he was far too inter-ested in what was happening on deck to have any time for reading.

It struck Ola that the Marquis was dif-ferent from what she would have expected of a man of his age and position.

She had heard so much about the riotous behaviour of the Bucks and Beaux in London that she imagined his life would be spent in search of pleasure and amusement.

Then she remembered that she had read of him in the Parliamentary Reports besides seeing his name mentioned continually on the sporting-pages of the newspapers.

'He obviously has many interests,' she thought to herself, and decided she would discuss them with him at dinner if she was still aboard.

The mere idea that she would soon be leaving brought back all the apprehensions and worries that had beset her in her cabin until she could not bear to think about them any more.

"I will manage, of course I will manage," she told herself reassuringly. "After all, it is not as though I have never been abroad before, although never . . . alone."

She knew it would be very different travelling on her own. When her father and mother had first taken her to the Convent they had stayed on the way with friends at their grand *Châteaux* and had made the journey an adventure which Ola knew she would never forget.

When she had returned to England with two other girls who were English, they had two Nuns in attendance and a Courier to arrange their rooms and see to the luggage.

'Now I shall be alone,' she thought, and she could not help shivering and feeling a little afraid.

She was convinced that it would be wisest to hire a post-chaise. But she still would have to stay at Inns on the way, and she thought that they would think it strange that a lady should be travelling alone, especially when she was so young.

A memory came flooding back to her

which was even more disturbing.

When she was returning to England with the Nuns, they had stopped at an Inn on the main Paris-to-Calais road. It was not large or as pleasant as the other Inns in which they had stayed, but, as the Nuns explained, it was the best available.

When they arrived it was to find that they were one room short, and while the Courier was arguing about it with the Proprietor, a woman had come up to the desk to speak to him and Ola had looked at her with interest.

She was French, with an extremely attractive face which also looked a little strange because, Ola realised, she used far more cosmetics than anyone she had ever seen before.

Her eye-lashes were mascaraed, her mouth was crimson, and there was definitely rouge on her cheeks.

Nevertheless, the clothes she wore were expensive and very elegant and she looked so pretty that Ola found it hard to understand why when she asked for a room the Proprietor's wife, who was attending to her while her husband was busy, said in a hard voice:

"Are you alone, *Madame?*"

"I have asked only for one room and that is the answer to your question," the lady replied.

"We do not let our rooms to women who travel alone," the Proprietor's wife had snapped. "You will find the type of Hotel you require farther down the street!"

She spoke in such a rude, uncompromising way that Ola expected the lady to reprimand her for her impertinence.

To her surprise, she merely shrugged her shoulders and walked out of the Hotel.

Now Ola wondered whether she, as a woman alone, would receive the same treatment.

She gave a little sigh at the thought, then told herself optimistically that at least there were some Hotels that would take women who travelled alone, and perhaps they would be quieter and less crowded.

The prospect of reaching Paris began to appear more difficult than she had thought at first, and there was so much to consider that, although she found several books which interested her amongst the Marquis's collection, while she was still thinking of her problems she fell asleep.

The Marquis, after an enjoyable two hours of watching his yacht plunge through the sea, came below, having learnt from the Captain that it would be impossible for them to turn towards Le Havre.

"The only thing I can suggest, M'Lord," he said, "is that we tack back there when the wind drops, but it will take time, and at this time of the year one can never be certain what the weather conditions will be like."

"No, we will go to Bordeaux as you suggested previously," the Marquis said. "I am sure Miss Milford, who is my guest, can easily find her way from there to Paris."

"Surely the young lady is not travelling all that way alone, M'Lord?" the Captain asked in surprise.

The Marquis was instantly annoyed that he had mentioned it and moved away without replying to the Captain's question.

"I have brought her to France as she asked," he told himself, "and I will not in any circumstances make her my responsibility!"

He remembered how Sarah had first evoked his sympathy because she seemed so helpless and pathetic without a husband to protect and care for her.

He saw now with a bitterness that seemed to run through his veins like poison that a great deal of it had been an act to make him feel big, strong, and protective.

He could recall the things she had said to him to which he had made the obvious reply! He could see all too clearly the trusting look in her eyes when she told him she was bewildered, worried, anxious, or upset. To which the inevitable answer was that he would see to it for her!

"Fool! Fool!" he told himself, and he felt the sound of the wind in the rigging repeat the same words.

"It is something I will never be again," he vowed.

When he went below he was seeking the words in which to tell Ola that the moment they reached Bordeaux his responsibility would be at an end.

"Whether she reaches Paris or anywhere else is nothing to do with me, and doubtless she will find plenty of other men to help her."

He wondered how many men there had been in Sarah's life besides Anthony.

There was no reason to think that he was the only one, and there must have been other men before her husband died!

Men who she found had been only too willing to look after and help a woman who pleaded with them with eyes as blue as a clear summer sky, but which were actually as dark with deceit as those of Satan himself.

The Marquis's eyes were hard and his lips were in a tight line as he entered the Saloon.

For a moment he thought that it was empty and Ola had retired to her own cabin. Then he saw that she was curled up on the sofa, asleep.

The Marquis had decorated the Saloon in pale green because it seemed an appropriate colour to use at sea.

That in itself had been revolutionary as most yachts were upholstered in brown leather and it was fashionable to have oak panelling on the cabin walls.

He could not have chosen a colour that was a more effective background for Ola's fiery red hair.

As the Marquis moved towards her he saw that her eye-lashes were very dark against her cheeks, which were still pale from tiredness, and in fact as she slept she looked very young and vulnerable.

He sat down on the chair opposite her, and it struck him that it was not surprising that she was tired, seeing what a dramatic day it had been for her yesterday.

Running away at dawn must have been a nerve-racking experience in itself. Then to learn of her cousin's intentions towards her had been a shock which was bad enough, without the sudden fright of an accident in the fog.

The Marquis had seen far too many accidents with carriage-horses not to be aware that Ola was lucky to have escaped unhurt.

Her cousin, who had been driving, had obviously been flung onto the road and it was unlikely, the Marquis thought, that the wound caused by the stone on which he had fallen would be his only injury.

Usually in such an accident he would have fractured a limb, while in several cases the Marquis was aware that people had broken their necks.

He wondered whether the horses were hurt, then told himself sharply that it was none of his business.

It was the brandy which was responsible for his having burdened himself with Ola and the sooner he was rid of her the better.

Then, looking at her, he wondered how, after he had put her ashore, she would reach Paris.

A post-chaise from Calais would not have been difficult, for it was the usual route taken by travellers, and the French with their shrewdness for making money had everything organised to suit the pockets of every class of person visiting their country.

But Bordeaux was a long way from Paris, and the Marquis began to think it might in fact be impossible for Ola to find a post-chaise to take her, even with a frequent change of horses, directly to Paris.

"I will not concern myself with her — I will not!" he said firmly.

Then he told himself that she was so young, a lady, and as such she was used to having servants, relatives, teachers and Governesses looking after her.

"She will find herself a Courier," a critical part of his mind told him, but then he wondered if a Courier of any repute would take on a woman who was by herself.

Moreover, there were Couriers who were known to prey on travellers, charging them exorbitant sums and even being in league with robbers who would relieve them of their luggage and other valuables before abandoning them penniless in some isolated part of the country.

'Damn her! Why did I ever meet her in the first place?' the Marquis thought to himself.

As the words were spoken in his mind, Ola opened her eyes.

For a moment she looked at him as if she wondered who he was. Then some memory came back to her and there was a smile on her lips that was very attractive as she sat up and said:

"I fell . . . asleep. I am ashamed of my indolence when I might have been improving my mind with one of your books."

"What you were doing was very sensible," the Marquis said. "It is extremely rough outside now. The wind is cold and there are gusts of sleet which are very unpleasant."

"All the same, you look as if you have enjoyed it!" Ola said. "Perhaps you will let me go on deck tomorrow."

"It depends if it is safe."

Ola gave a little sigh.

"I believe you are afraid I shall break my leg, and then you will not be able to be rid of me unless you throw me overboard!"

What she was saying was so near to what the Marquis was thinking that he felt almost embarrassed.

He did not reply and Ola said:

"I promise you I will go ashore the moment you tell me to do so, but there is one thing I want to ask you."

"What is that?"

"As we are going to Bordeaux and it is a town I have never visited and therefore know very little about, do you think there is a good jeweller there?"

"A jeweller?" the Marquis asked in perplexity. "What do you want with a jeweller?"

It flashed through his mind that she might be expecting him to give her a present. He remembered so many women who had somehow lured him into a jeweller's so that he could demonstrate his affection for them in what to them was a very much more practical manner than by kisses.

Ola looked down, as if she was shy, then said in a small voice:

"I think . . . if I could have got off at . . . Calais . . . I would have had enough . . . money to reach Paris . . . but as Bordeaux is so much . . . farther away . . . I shall have to . . . sell some of my jewellery . . . and I do not wish to be . . . defrauded."

"Surely you did not set off from home without having enough money to carry you to Paris?" the Marquis asked. "How much did you bring?"

There was silence and he had a feeling that she was not going to tell him the truth.

"Do not lie to me!" he said sharply. "Quite frankly, I am not really interested in your finances one way or another. If you want my help you had better at least be honest."

"I . . . I was not going to . . . lie," Ola replied. "I just did not wish you to think I was . . . foolish to bring so little money with me."

"How much have you got?"

"F-four sovereigns . . . and some . . . silver."

Before the Marquis could speak she added quickly:

"Because Giles was coming with me . . . I thought it would be . . . enough."

"So you intended that he should pay for you, even before you learnt he wished to marry you?" the Marquis asked scornfully.

"Not at all!" Ola answered. "He knew that as Step-Mama has the handling of my fortune she could pay him back anything I owed him . . . or else I would have given him a piece of . . . Mama's jewellery. It is very valuable!"

"And you mean to say you are carrying it all in that case you had with you last night?"

Ola nodded.

"My dear child," the Marquis said, "do you really imagine you can reach Paris without having it stolen from you and perhaps being knocked about or killed in the process?"

"There is . . . nothing else I . . . can do," Ola said defensively.

She gave a little cry.

"Oh, it is easy for you to find fault and say: 'You should have known better!' now that everything has gone wrong, but I trusted Giles when he said he would take me to the Convent. Now last night I thought of . . . something . . . else."

"What is that?" the Marquis asked in an unsympathetic tone.

"Because Giles knows where I intended to go, he will, when he is better, look for me there . . . so I cannot now stay at the . . . Convent."

The Marquis looked at her.

"Then where do you intend to go?"

"I have not yet decided."

"But you have to go somewhere."

"Yes, I know, but there is no reason for me to worry you with my plans. You have made it quite clear that I am not your responsibility, which of course I am not."

"No, of course not," the Marquis agreed. "At the same time, shall I say I am curious! You did mention an alternative last night, I think."

"Yes. I told you that Step-Mama was always saying I would have to be a cocotte but that I was not certain exactly what that means."

She looked at the Marquis as if he could supply the answer. When he did not do so, she went on:

"I looked the word up in the French dictionary, and it said: *'Fille de joie'* — 'woman of joy,' and I thought that must mean an actress of some sort. Is that not so?"

"Not exactly," the Marquis replied.

"I expect they will tell me what it is when I get to Paris. The trouble is, I can hardly walk down the street asking for an Instructor on how to be a *'Fille de joie'*! Perhaps they would be able to tell me at a Theatre?"

She gave him a mischievous little smile as she went on:

"The Nuns would be very shocked! They thought Theatres were the invention of the Devil and always warned us against visiting them, although we were allowed occasionally to attend the Opera House."

The Marquis was finding it almost impossible to know what he could say to this ridiculous, ignorant child. He made up his mind.

"The best thing I can do," he said firmly, "is to sail to Plymouth. There I will engage a responsible Courier who will take you back to your Stepmother."

Even before he had finished speaking Ola gave a cry of horror that seemed to echo round the cabin.

"How can you suggest anything so abominable, so cruel, so treacherous?" she cried. "You know I cannot go back to my Stepmother, and you have no authority to send me."

She paused to catch her breath.

"I called you a Good Samaritan, but you are a *wolf* in sheep's clothing and your yacht is aptly named . . . you are a *sea wolf* and I hate you!"

As she spoke he rose from his chair, and without looking at her, moved towards the door. It would have been a dignified exit except that a sudden movement of the ship made him stagger, and it was only with the greatest difficulty that he prevented himself from falling.

When he had gone, Ola stared despairingly at the door as if she could not believe that she had heard him aright.

He had seemed so kind, so helpful, and she had thought at luncheon-time, apart from anything else, how interesting it would be to talk to him.

Now suddenly for no reason he had turned against her and was behaving as badly in his way as Giles had behaved in his.

"How dare he! How dare he treat me as if I were a child to be taken here or there without even being consulted!" she cried aloud.

She wanted to scream in defiance at the Marquis, and yet at the same time her instinct told her that, sea wolf or not, it would be best for her to plead with him.

Then she knew by the tone of his voice and the squareness of his chin that he meant what he said and she would find it hard to dissuade him from doing what he intended.

'If he sends me home,' she thought, 'I shall have to run away all over again and it will be more difficult another time.'

She had the feeling too that the Marquis would make sure that she did not escape while she was with him, and she wished now that she had not entrusted her jewellery to him.

She thought she now hated the Marquis as much as she hated Giles.

'Men are all the same,' she thought. 'They do not play fairly unless it suits their own ends.'

She wondered why the girls at School were always talking of men as if they were something marvellous and more desirable than anything else on earth.

"I hate men!" Ola told herself. "I hate them as I hate my Stepmother! All I want to do is to live by myself and be allowed to have friends and do all the things I want to do without being ordered about by anybody!"

It had occurred to her a long time ago that when one was married one would always be at the beck and call of some man who thought he had authority over her.

Perhaps that would be endurable if one was in love, but otherwise it would be intolerable. She thought that because she was rich, she need be in no hurry to get married but could wait until she found somebody whom she would like to live with simply because he was kind and understanding and she would be able to talk to him.

She had often thought in the past that it was difficult to find people to whom she could talk when she was at the Convent.

The Nuns gave orders, and when she was with her father he talked to her but he did not converse. In fact, neither he nor anybody else was interested in her opinions or her ideas.

'When I talked to the Marquis at luncheon,' she thought, 'he listened to me when I was describing the different ships in which I have sailed in the past, and he explained the things I wanted to know about his own yacht.'

From the number of books in his bookcase it struck her that he was interested in a great number of subjects about which she wished to know more.

'We will talk about them tonight at dinner,' she had thought excitedly, but now he had made it very clear what he thought of her.

She was an unwanted piece of merchandise of which he would dispose as he saw fit, without even asking her opinion on the matter.

'I hate him!' she thought. 'I hate him because he has deceived me when I thought he was kind and honest.'

She did not want to cry when she thought of her future; it only made her angry.

Somehow, in some way, she would get even with the Marquis because he had disappointed her when she had least expected it.

"I am glad he is upset about something, and I hope a woman has really hurt him and made him unhappy!" she said to herself. "It will serve him right! If he ever told me about it I would laugh because I am pleased he has been made to suffer!"

This was all very well, but it did not solve her own problem and she told herself that now she had to escape somehow.

There seemed no possibility of her doing anything of the sort unless she was prepared to throw herself into the sea.

"If I do so," she mused, "I should be drowned and perhaps it would be on his conscience for the rest of his life."

Then she told herself sensibly that he would merely attribute it to an unbalanced mind and forget all about it long before he reached the Mediterranean.

But Ola was not going to be defeated.

She sat back against the cushions and

began to plan how she could elude the Marquis and his ideas in one way or another.

'Perhaps if I stow away in the hold,' she thought, 'he will think I have gone ashore and I shall only be discovered when he is out at sea again.'

It seemed quite a possible idea, except that she had the feeling he would make very sure that the Courier he engaged acted as a jailor too and there would be no escape at least until he was too far away even to know about it.

"What am I to do? What *am* I to do?" Ola asked herself.

Then as there was a sudden rasp of the wind in the rigging which told her that there was still a gale outside, it occurred to her that perhaps the Marquis's intentions would be circumvented not by her but by nature and they would not be able to dock in Plymouth as he intended.

CHAPTER FOUR

Ola was sitting on her bed, an expression of despair on her face.

She had learnt from the steward that the *Sea Wolf* would dock in Plymouth either very late tonight or first thing in the morning, depending on the wind and the tides.

In the last twelve hours she had thought of nothing except how she could escape from the Marquis and prevent him from sending her ignominiously back to her Stepmother.

She had been sensible enough not to rage at him when they had luncheon together, but instead to talk about the races and horses which took part in them.

She knew he was surprised that she was not referring to what lay ahead, but after a little stiffness at the beginning of the meal he gradually relaxed and talked to her as if she were as knowledgeable as he was on the subject.

Every hour that passed brought her nearer to her fate, and she thought now that even her optimism was fading and there would be nothing she could do but leave the

Marquis and set off on her homeward journey with the jailor he would provide for her.

There was a knock on the door and Ola started.

"Come in!" she said, and the steward who always looked after her stood there.

" 'Scuse me, Miss," he said, "but do you happen to have any laudanum with you? The Captain's got such an aching tooth that he can't stay on deck."

"Oh! I am sorry," Ola exclaimed, "and I wish I could help, but laudanum is something I never take myself."

The steward smiled.

"You're too young, if I may say so, Miss, for such fads and fancies, but there was just a chance, and the Captain's groaning in his bunk like a lost soul."

Ola could not help smiling. Then she said:

"Tell him to soak a little wool or a rag in spirit . . . brandy is best, although I daresay rum would do . . . and pack it round it, if possible into the tooth that is hurting. I remember my father doing that once."

"I'll tell the Captain what you said, Miss," the steward replied. "I know he'll be very grateful."

He shut the cabin door and as he did so

Ola gave a little exclamation.

She suddenly remembered that she might have some laudanum with her after all.

When she had left the Convent many of the girls of her age had given her presents and among them had been a beautiful chinoiserie enamel scent-holder made in the reign of Louis XIV.

It was very attractive and when she opened it she found it contained three little bottles shaped like triangles so that they fitted together to make a whole.

They each had enamelled stoppers and their glass was engraved with flowers.

Yvonne, the girl who had given them to her, had said:

"I have put the most exotic perfume I could find in one, an *eau-de-toilette* in the second, and you will have to fill the third yourself."

Ola had never actually used the bottles, but, because it was so attractive, the case had stood on her dressing-table, and when she was packing, thinking that she might see her friend when she was in France, she had put it at the bottom of her trunk.

She had not thought of it until now, but actually the third bottle contained laudanum.

Soon after she had returned from Paris

she had suffered from the most acute tooth-ache which turned out to be an abscess.

The Doctor had been called to see her and he had promised to arrange for a Dentist to visit her the following day.

"Because I know what pain you're in, Miss Milford," he said, "I'm going to give you a little laudanum to take tonight so that you will sleep. Be careful not to take too much."

He had handed her a small bottle as he spoke and instructed her to take only a few drops.

It had certainly helped her to bear the pain, and when her tooth no longer hurt, Ola, thinking that the medicine-bottle looked untidy, had tipped what remained of the laudanum into the empty bottle in her chinoiserie case.

"How stupid of me!" she said aloud. "Of course I can help the Captain!"

She opened her trunk which she had already filled with her clothes, feeling that if she did not do so the Marquis would be informed and would think it was a deliberate act of defiance.

In the bottom corner she found, as she expected, the enamel case carefully wrapped in cotton-wool to protect it.

She drew it out and rose to her feet to call

the steward so that he could take it to the Captain.

Even as her hand went out towards the door, she paused.

An idea had come to her, an idea that was so fantastic that she told herself it was impossible and would be quite unworkable.

And yet, fascinated by it, she sat down on the bed to consider it carefully, step by step.

Wearing a very attractive gown and, because it was cold, a fur wrap round her shoulders, Ola was waiting in the Saloon when the Marquis came in to dinner.

Each night, despite the roughness of the weather, he changed into his evening-clothes, and he looked to Ola as elegant and impressive as if he were going to a dinner-party in London rather than dining alone with her.

"Good-evening, Ola!" he said. "I think the wind is dropping a little, and certainly the *Sea Wolf* is travelling more smoothly than she was yesterday."

"I have found that," Ola smiled. "But my elbows are black and blue from having to support me as I was thrown against the cabin walls."

"You should have stayed in bed!" the Marquis said automatically.

"That would be an admission of defeat, which I most dislike acknowledging at any time!"

He gave her a sharp glance, as if he thought she was referring to other things than the movement of the sea.

She quickly turned the conversation to the subject she wished to discuss with him but had not yet had the opportunity.

"I found in your bookcase a volume of Hansard," she said, "and I see that you made a speech in the House of Lords regarding the employment of young children in factories and coal-mines."

"You read it?" the Marquis asked in surprise.

"I only wish I could have heard it. It is something about which I feel very strongly, as every woman should."

It struck the Marquis that no woman he had known in the past had been in the slightest degree interested either in his speeches or in the children, as young as four and five, who were made to work sometimes as much as twelve hours a day and who were beaten if they fell asleep.

For a moment he thought that Ola was only toadying to him and would start pleading with him not to send her back to her Stepmother.

To his surprise, she not only talked with unmistakable sincerity on the subject, but she also had obviously read quite a lot of the reports which had been published in the newspapers besides being discussed in Parliament.

They argued over the rights and wrongs of employing child-labour and also as to what compensation could be given to the employers if it was forbidden.

The Marquis found himself waxing very eloquent about what he intended to bring before the House of Lords in the future, and he discovered that Ola was also interested in the Reform Bill.

"Is it true," she asked, "that the King scrawled on a piece of paper:

" 'I consider Dissolution
Tantamount to Revolution.' "

"Who told you that?" the Marquis enquired.

"I must have read it somewhere, but I cannot believe, old though he is, that the King does not realise that reforms are necessary."

"The trouble is," the Marquis replied, "he has a rooted dislike of elections and only with difficulty made up his mind to dissolve Parliament. I think too, as he is really a simple sailor, he finds the Bill in all its complexity very difficult to understand."

"I have always been sure," Ola said, "that he has not the brilliant brain of his brother, the late King George IV."

"That is true," the Marquis agreed, "but, though I am fond of His Majesty, I cannot help sometimes remembering that Greville wrote: 'He is but a plain, vulgar, hospitable gentleman, opening his doors to all the world with a frightful Queen and a posse of bastards.'"

As he spoke, he realised to whom he was speaking and said quickly:

"I apologise."

"No, please do not do that," Ola said. "I like to be talked to as if I were your equal rather than a foolish, unfledged girl without a brain in her head."

"I would certainly never say that about you," the Marquis replied.

A steward cleared the table but left a decanter of brandy and one of claret in front of the Marquis.

They were ship's decanters, made so that it was impossible to upset them or to turn them over as they had very broad bases and were of extremely heavy cut crystal.

Ola looked at them for a minute, then she said:

"As this is our last dinner together, My Lord, I would like to propose a toast."

The Marquis raised his eye-brows; then, feeling that as she was trying to be pleasant he must do the same, he replied:

"I shall join with pleasure in any toast you suggest, Ola. Will you drink claret or brandy?"

"I think claret," she replied, "but only a very little."

The Marquis half-filled the glass in front of her.

"I shall join you," he said, and filled his own.

Ola reached for her glass but as she moved she gave a little cry.

"Oh, my brooch!" she exclaimed. "I could not have fastened it properly and I heard it fall beneath the table."

As she spoke she dropped the diamond brooch she held in her hand down beside the hem of her skirt.

"How foolish of me," she said. "I should not have worn it, but it looked so pretty with this gown."

"I will pick it up," the Marquis said.

He pushed back his chair, looked down, and saw that the brooch was out of reach of his hands unless he went down on his knees.

As he did so, Ola bent forward to tip into

the Marquis's glass of claret the contents of the little cut-glass bottle she had hidden beside her.

She had emptied it by the time he retrieved the brooch and emerged from under the table to sit in his chair again.

"There you are," he said.

As he held out the diamond brooch towards her, he said:

"It is certainly a very beautiful piece of jewellery."

Ola smiled.

"It was one of my mother's smaller brooches. My father loved her so much and gave her magnificent jewels on every possible occasion and anniversary!"

"Then you must keep it safe," the Marquis admonished, "and if you sell it, be careful that you are not defrauded."

"I will be," Ola said, taking the brooch from him.

She set it down on the table and lifted her glass.

"To the *Sea Wolf*!" she said. "May she find, wherever she sails, new horizons and eventually happiness!"

"A charming toast, Ola!" the Marquis exclaimed.

She knew he was surprised not only at the words but at the sincere way in which she had spoken them.

She smiled at him and the smile seemed to illuminate her face.

"No heel-taps," she said, and lifted her glass to her lips.

Because he was prepared to humour her, the Marquis tipped the entire contents of his glass down his throat.

But when he had swallowed and put his glass down on the table there was a frown on his forehead.

"I thought — that wine tasted — a little strange . . ." he began.

He reached out his hand as if he would take hold of the decanter, but before he could do so he leant back in his chair as if the effort was too great and after a second or so shut his eyes.

Ola watched him anxiously.

She knew she had given him a very large dose of laudanum, and she was not certain how soon it would act and whether he would have time to call a steward to his assistance.

It was soon obvious that he would not do so, though quite a long time passed while he sat with closed eyes before his head fell to one side and she knew he was asleep.

Fortunately, the chair in which he was sitting, which was battened to the deck, had a wing-back and his head rested against one of the wings, so that Ola knew it would be impossible for anybody coming through the door to know whether he was awake or asleep.

Just as she had planned, because she felt that the steward outside would be listening in case he was required, she went on talking.

Because she did not dare try to imitate the Marquis's voice, she made deep humming noises when he should have spoken, which made it sound, she hoped, as if he were speaking in a lower tone than she was.

After ten minutes had passed she rang the gold bell that stood on the table.

As she had guessed, the steward had been waiting outside, and as he opened the door she said in an excited tone, as if she were speaking to the Marquis:

"Oh, let me send the order! It is so wonderful of you! I am so happy!"

Then she turned her face towards the steward who stood just inside the door.

"Will you inform the Captain or the First Mate, if he is now in charge of the yacht," she said, "that His Lordship says that as the weather is better we will not now put into Plymouth as arranged, but will sail with all possible speed towards the South."

She was obviously so delighted with the command and her pleasure was so infectious that as she smiled at the end of what she had to say, the steward smiled back.

"I'll give the order to the First Mate right away, Miss," he said, and went from the Saloon, closing the door.

Ola went on talking as she had done before, lowering her voice to impersonate the Marquis's responses.

Then she lifted the decanter of claret and, moving from the table, poured the contents down behind the sofa.

As that piece of furniture was also battened down, she knew that the wine was most unlikely ever to be discovered since it would seep into the wood and be practically indiscernible.

Then she put the empty decanter back on the table and went on talking.

Nearly an hour later she rang the bell for the second time, and when the steward answered she said in a hesitating and rather nervous little voice:

"His Lordship has fallen . . . asleep . . . I think perhaps he is . . . very tired."

The steward came quickly to the table and Ola saw him glance at the empty decanter before he said:

"I'll fetch Gibson, Miss. I expects you'd like to go to your own cabin."

"I think that would be a good idea," Ola agreed, "and thank you very much."

A little later she heard the Marquis being carried towards the Master Suite, which was past her cabin door.

When she got into bed she knew with a little leap of her heart that she had got the better of the Marquis!

"At least by the time he wakes it will be too late to go back to Plymouth," she told herself.

She shut her eyes, determined that she would not worry as to what would happen when the Marquis awoke, but would try to sleep.

The Marquis stirred, feeling as if his head were filled with fog, and had a fleeting memory of walking through the darkness to the *Sea Wolf*.

He opened his eyes with an effort and somebody rose from the other side of the cabin and came towards him.

"If you're awake, M'Lord, I thinks Your Lordship should have something to drink," he heard Gibson say, and felt a glass pressed against his lips.

He took a few sips, then turned away petulantly to say in a thick voice:

"Leave — me alone — I am — tired!"

When he awoke again he was aware that

there was sunshine coming through the port-holes and now his head felt clearer although his mouth was dry.

Once again Gibson came to his side, and this time he asked:

"What is the time? Where are we?"

"Sailing down the coast of Portugal, M'Lord."

It took the Marquis a moment to understand what had been said. Then with an effort, clutching at his memory, which seemed to be trying to escape him, he said:

"Portugal? You mean — Plymouth!"

"No, M'Lord. Portugal! We're already well past the Bay of Biscay."

The Marquis forced his mind to assimilate this information. Then in a voice that was a little stronger he asked:

"What the devil are we doing here? I gave orders to dock at Plymouth!"

"I understand you countermanded that order, M'Lord, and told the Captain to sail South as quickly as possible. We've had the wind behind us all the way and it's been the best passage I've ever known in the Bay. It's a pity Your Lordship weren't awake to appreciate it!"

There was silence for a moment, then the Marquis asked:

"Are you telling me that I have been

asleep since before we were due to reach Plymouth?"

"Yes, M'Lord. I've never known Your Lordship sleep like it," Gibson replied. "And I've never known claret, not even a whole decanter, to have such an effect."

"I was drunk?" the Marquis enquired.

"I'm afraid so, M'Lord. And it's the first time I've seen Your Lordship so 'foxed'!"

"How long have I been in this state?"

"Three days, M'Lord!"

"I do not believe it!"

The Marquis forced himself to sit up in bed.

"Three days!" he said as if he was speaking to himself. "And you think that is possible on one bottle of claret?"

"Your Lordship had nothing else," Gibson replied defensively. "The stewards said that the brandy went untouched."

"I slept for three days on one bottle of claret?"

"There must have been two," Gibson conceded. "What Your Lordship drank at dinner, and a full decanter placed on the table after dinner."

Because the Marquis was sitting up it seemed that his head was swimming dizzily, so he lay back again.

"There is something wrong here, Gibson," he said. "Very wrong! I intend, when I am better, to get to the bottom of it."

"Yes, M'Lord, of course, M'Lord," Gibson agreed, "but Your Lordship should rest until you feel yourself again."

The Marquis was silent for a moment. Then as his valet was moving away from the bed he said:

"The young lady — what is her name?"

"Miss Milford, M'Lord."

"She is still aboard?"

"Yes, M'Lord. Enjoying every moment of the voyage. Up on deck from first thing in the morning to last thing at night. We've all been saying we've never seen a young lady so happy."

The Marquis lay still.

Now he was remembering what had happened.

He had been firm in his decision to put Ola ashore at Plymouth and send her back to her Stepmother so that he would no longer have any responsibility for her.

He remembered too how at first she had raged at him and accused him of treachery. Then she had been surprisingly pleasant, especially at dinner.

Slowly, because it was an effort, he tried to recall everything that had been said, everything that had happened.

Now he remembered the toast she had asked him to drink and how after he had poured a little claret into her glass and filled his own she had dropped her diamond brooch under the table.

He had retrieved it, then she had thanked him and had lifted her glass, saying:

"No heel-taps!"

He gave a little exclamation.

It was after he had drunk his glass of claret, and had thought it had a strange taste, that darkness had covered him and he remembered no more.

The Marquis was extremely intelligent, and although it seemed incredible that this sort of thing, like something out of a Walter Scott novel, could happen in real life, he felt sure that when he was picking up her brooch Ola by some means had drugged his wine!

But was she likely to carry a drug round with her? he wondered.

Then, knowing how he had felt when he first awoke, the heaviness of his head and the difficulty he had thinking, it struck him that he had felt like this once before.

It was after he had broken his collar-bone out hunting and the Doctor had been called to attend to him at Elvin. He had hurt him excruciatingly when he had put the bone back into place.

He had cursed and the Doctor had opened his leather bag and produced a small bottle, and from it he had poured some dark liquid into a teaspoon.

"Drink this, My Lord."

"What is it?" the Marquis had enquired.

"Only laudanum, but it will take the edge off the pain."

"Women's remedy!" the Marquis had said scornfully.

"Women are not expected to be courageous about pain like a man," the Doctor had replied, "but I have always believed there is no point in suffering unnecessarily."

"No, you are right," the Marquis had agreed.

He had taken the laudanum and found it helped him considerably, though the next morning he awoke with a heavy head and a dry mouth such as he had now.

Of course that was what Ola had given him — laudanum — and he told himself that he had been a fool not to be suspicious of what she was up to when she had made herself so pleasant and talked so agreeably to him.

He had known that she was determined not to return to her Stepmother, just as he was determined that she should.

'Damn the woman — she has won!' the

Marquis thought irritably.

He slept intermittently for the rest of the day, and every time he was conscious he found himself growing more and more angry that Ola had managed to trick him.

But there was in fact nothing he could do at the moment but take her along with him to the Mediterranean.

He supposed that they were now long past Lisbon.

The next civilised port-of-call would be Gibraltar, and as that was a British possession there would be far too many explanations if the Marquis of Elvington left an attractive but very young woman stranded there while he sailed on alone.

'I suppose I can put her ashore at Marseilles or Nice,' he thought, and wondered whether, if he told her what he intended, she would find another means of circumventing his plans.

After a good night's sleep he felt remarkably well and in comparatively good spirits, except that he was still angry with Ola.

When he was dressed he went up on deck, and now he no longer needed an overcoat or oil-skins, for the sun was warm and the sea reflected the blue of the sky.

"Good-morning, M'Lord!" the Captain said as soon as he appeared. "I hope Your

Lordship's in better health?"

The Marquis bit back the angry retort that there had been nothing wrong with his health except that he had been drugged without being aware of it.

But he knew it would be undignified to say anything of the sort, so he merely replied:

"I am sorry to have missed so much of the voyage, Captain. Gibson told me this morning that we have had the best passage he has ever known through the Bay."

"Fantastic, M'Lord!" the Captain replied. "The wind exactly right, the sea dropping after the storm, and I already feel as if the winter is over and we've found the spring."

"Yes, indeed," the Marquis agreed, feeling that the Captain was being quite poetic.

Because he looked surprised, the Captain said with an apologetic smile:

"Those are not my words, M'Lord, but Miss Milford's. We've all been thinking she looks like spring herself, and no mistake!"

The Marquis followed the direction of the Captain's eyes and saw Ola, whom he had not noticed before.

She was sitting on deck, protected by a piece of superstructure and looking, although he hated to admit it, very spring-like and undeniably beautiful.

She wore no hat and the lights in her red hair seemed to dance in the sunlight, her eyes were deep green like the waves as they broke against the bow of the ship, and her skin was dazzlingly white.

As she saw him looking at her she raised her hand in a wave and the smile on her lips seemed to welcome him.

He wondered how she dared to appear so unselfconscious about her misdeeds, but he told himself that this was not the moment to confront her with them.

He therefore made no effort to move towards her but stood talking to the Captain. As he watched the ship move with a speed that thrilled him, it was hard, despite himself, to continue to be in a bad humour.

"There's a little damage I would like to speak to you about, M'Lord," the Captain said, after the Marquis had been silent for some time.

"Damage?"

"Nothing very serious, M'Lord, but in the storm two of the water-butts broke loose and knocked against each other, spilling their contents."

"Two?" the Marquis asked sharply.

"They've been repaired, M'Lord, and as good as they ever were, but they are empty and I wondered if Your Lordship would consider putting into a bay I know of, a bit further down the coast, where there's a spring of sweet, clear water."

"You have been there before?" the Marquis asked.

"Twice, M'Lord. Once in the war when I was serving in a Brig and we were out of water completely, and we filled up there and very glad we were of it too. The second time was when I was on Lord Lutworth's yacht, M'Lord. Very mean, His Lordship was, and though I told him the water-butts were not sea-worthy he wouldn't listen to me. Fell to bits, they did, when we encountered a storm off the southern coast of Portugal."

"That was unfortunate," the Marquis remarked.

"Soon, M'Lord, there wasn't a single drop of water left in the whole ship."

"That certainly must not happen to us," the Marquis said, "so we will drop anchor in your bay, Captain. How long before we get there?"

"About forty-eight hours, M'Lord; and you might like to stretch your legs on shore."

"It is certainly an idea," the Marquis agreed.

All the time he was talking he was acutely

aware that Ola was watching him, and now, almost as if she was compelling him, he walked along the deck.

"I want to speak to you, Ola!" he said when he reached her.

He saw the light go out of her eyes as she asked:

"Here, or in the Saloon?"

"In the Saloon," he replied, and went below without waiting to assist her.

She joined him a few minutes later, and as she came into the Saloon he saw that the expression in her eyes was apprehensive even though her hair seemed like a flag of defiance.

She did not wait for him to speak but moved across the cabin to sit down on the sofa she usually occupied, saying as she did so:

"I am sorry . . . very sorry . . . I know you are . . . angry with me."

"What did you expect me to be?" the Marquis asked.

"I had to save myself from my Stepmother . . . and it was the only way I could . . . do so."

"What did you give me?"

"Laudanum."

"How much?"

"I am afraid . . . nearly a whole bottle . . . it was only a small bottle . . . but I knew it was . . . a very strong dose."

"You might have killed me!" the Marquis said sharply.

"There was really no chance of that," Ola replied, "but you did sleep for a long time. I was glad when we reached the coast of Portugal."

"I suppose you realise that your behaviour is so outrageous, so incredible, that I find it difficult to express what I feel about it?"

"I have said I am sorry," Ola answered, "but it was the only way I could prevent you from sending me home unless I threw myself overboard. I did seriously think of . . . that."

"You do not frighten me with your dramatics."

"I know that, and as I have abused your hospitality I am prepared to leave when we reach the South of France."

"That is certainly very kind of you," the Marquis said sarcastically, "and I suppose you will be up against the same difficulties as before — no money and nowhere to go."

"I have told you . . . I will go to Paris."

"Oh, for God's sake!" he said in an irritable tone. "We cannot go over all that again. For the moment we had best talk of something else, otherwise I shall feel inclined to give you the beating you thoroughly deserve."

She gave a little exclamation but she did not speak, and the Marquis went on:

"It is obviously a punishment that was neglected when you were young, and your over-fertile imagination was given too much licence."

He spoke not angrily but in the bitter, sarcastic tone that Ola thought was almost as wounding as if he actually used the whip with which he had threatened her.

Then suddenly as she thought of how she should reply to him she gave a little chuckle.

"It was clever of me, was it not?" she asked. "I despaired . . . I really despaired of how I could prevent you from putting me ashore at Plymouth. Then the steward asked me if I had any laudanum with me as the Captain had a tooth-ache."

"And you refused to help the Captain?"

"I refused because I had actually forgotten I had it in my trunk," Ola answered. "Then I remembered it and suddenly thought of a way to prevent you from sending me home from Plymouth and to contrive that you should take me South with you."

She saw the steel in his eyes and put out her hand impulsively on his arm.

"Please . . . please forgive me . . . and let us go on talking together as we did before. It was so exciting for me . . . so different from

. . . anything I have enjoyed before, and although I know you will not admit it . . . you seemed to . . . enjoy it too."

The Marquis looked at the pleading in her green eyes, and despite his resolution to remain firm and very annoyed, he found himself weakening.

"I am extremely angry with you," he said, "but I suppose there is nothing I can do but accept this ridiculous situation, which incidentally is extremely reprehensible from the point of view of your reputation."

"I stopped worrying about my reputation long ago," Ola replied, "and who is to know or to care where I am, except my Stepmother, who will only be afraid that I shall be found, which will prevent her from keeping my fortune all to herself."

"It is your fortune, as you call it, that is at the bottom of all this trouble," the Marquis said.

"Of course it is, and I was thinking that if Papa had had a son I should not be so rich and then no-one would have worried about me," Ola said. "Let that be a lesson to you! When you have a family, have lots of children, not just one tiresome daughter."

"I can simplify things far more easily than that," the Marquis said, "by not getting married and not having any children."

He spoke bitterly and without thinking, simply because the word "marriage" made him remember Sarah once again.

As he did so, it struck him that in the days when he had been unconscious, and today when he was himself, he had not once thought of her.

"I have decided never to marry too," Ola said confidingly. "I have been ordered about too much in my life, and a husband might easily be worse than my Stepmother, worse than Giles, and worse than you!"

"You cannot spend the rest of your life alone!" the Marquis remarked.

"I shall make friends," Ola replied, "and friends are easier to dispense with than relatives and husbands."

"You are talking nonsense!" the Marquis snapped. "Of course you will have to marry, and the quicker the better, so that you will have a man to look after you."

"And order me about?"

"Undoubtedly, and, what is more, you will have to obey him."

"I refuse, I absolutely refuse!"

Then she was smiling at him mischievously as she said:

"Although I daresay I shall manage to do what I want to do, one way or another."

"I can quite believe that, and your future

husband will have all my sympathy."

He saw her eyes twinkle and had the feeling that she was not taking him seriously and was in fact so relieved that he was not really angry with her that she was laughing at his helplessness.

"You are an extremely irritating brat!" he said. "God knows what will happen to you in your life, but I refuse to let it worry me."

He reached out for the bell and rang it.

"I am going to have a glass of champagne," he said. "Would you like to join me?"

"It sounds very luxurious and exciting," Ola said, "especially for me."

"You must have had champagne before?"

"Yes, but not at sea in a magnificent yacht with a handsome nobleman all to myself!" Ola replied. "What could be a better opening to a dramatic story of adventure and romance?"

For a moment the Marquis glared at her, then found himself laughing.

He was right, she was incorrigible, and there was nothing he could do about it.

He had never in his life expected to encounter a woman who could behave in so outrageous a manner and yet make him laugh at her behaviour.

"A bottle of champagne!" he said to the steward.

When the champagne came, the steward opened it in front of him and poured a glass for the Marquis and one for Ola.

When the man had left the cabin the Marquis said:

"I have no intention of taking my eyes off this glass before I drink it, so if you drop anything on the floor you can pick it up yourself."

"I was so afraid," Ola admitted, "that you would be too grand to lower yourself and would ring for a steward to find my brooch, in which case everything would have been much more difficult."

"It is something I shall remember to do in the future," the Marquis said, "especially if there is someone like you about."

"You are quite safe now where I am concerned. I would never do such an unimaginative thing as to perform the same trick twice."

"You are not going to play any more tricks on me," the Marquis said. "Let us make that quite certain, otherwise I swear I will throw you overboard!"

"I warn you, I can swim!" Ola retorted. "And I shall either reach the shore or wait for another yacht to come by, which, with my good luck, will contain a handsome, wealthy, unmarried Duke. I intend to go one higher each time!"

The Marquis laughed again.

"Perhaps we should confine ourselves to a quieter, less eventful life, at least until we reach the South of France."

There was silence, until Ola asked in a rather small voice:

"Then what are you . . . going to . . . do with . . . me?"

"I have not yet decided," the Marquis replied, "but of course a lot will rest on your behaviour in the meantime."

"Then I will be good," Ola said, "very, very good, and perhaps if I am . . ."

She paused before she said quickly:

"No, I will not say it. It might be unlucky."

"You are right, it might be terribly unlucky," the Marquis agreed, "but you are to promise me that there will be no more tricks, and you have to swear that you have no drugs, poisons, or lethal weapons of any sort hidden in your possessions."

"Very well then, I promise," Ola said. "And do you know what I have been doing while you were asleep?"

"What?" the Marquis asked in an uncompromising voice.

"I have been reading about the Reform Bill. I found quite a lot of papers about it in a drawer in your desk."

She looked up at him quickly as she asked:

"You do not mind my looking for them and reading them?"

"I presume, as I am allowed to have no privacy where you are concerned, that I have to accept your somewhat high-handed methods. I realise that nothing is sacred from your curiosity."

"If I had found any love-letters or anything like that," Ola said, "I would of course not have thought of opening them or reading them, but printed leaflets are different. I could see quite clearly what they were."

The Marquis gave up the hopeless task of explaining that he did not expect his guests, whoever they might be, to rifle the drawers in his desk.

Instead he said:

"I should be interested to hear your opinion on what has been proposed so far in the amendments which I expect you have read and which were included in the Second Bill."

"Quite frankly, I did not think they went far enough," Ola said.

Then, almost despite himself, the Marquis found himself defending the Government and refuting Ola's contention of "too little and too late" as if he were speaking to a man of his own age.

CHAPTER FIVE

The *Sea Wolf* sailed into a small bay sur-rounded by high cliffs.

They peaked so high that they looked like mountains rising from a small sandy beach, and Ola, watching every movement, ex-claimed with delight when the anchor went down.

"What an ideal place!" she said to the Marquis. "I do wish we could swim in this clear water."

"I am afraid you would find it very cold," he said, "and the sea can be very treach-erous at this time of the year."

"There is always some excuse for my not doing what I want to do," Ola pouted, and he laughed.

"I do not intend to feel sorry for you," he said. "You get your own way far too much already."

She gave him a mischievous glance from under her eye-lashes, and he knew that she was being provocative in a manner which he had grown used to yet still found alternately irritating and intriguing.

The sailors had already lowered the boat

into the water, and as Ola and the Marquis climbed down a rope-ladder into it, other men were bringing the empty water-butts up from below-decks.

"I want to see the spring," Ola said as they were rowed away towards the shore.

They went to the spring first, and it was in fact rather disappointing to look at.

There was only a small amount of water flowing from the dark rock, but when they tasted it the Marquis knew that the Captain had been right in saying it was both pure and clear.

"If we were enterprising," Ola said, "we would start a Spa here and sell the water to people with ailments, most of which I am convinced are imaginary."

"I think the Spanish might object to that," the Marquis replied with a smile.

They moved away from the spring, and as they walked over the soft golden sand, Ola looked up at the cliffs rising above and said:

"Think what a wonderful view there must be from the top, not only over to the sea but over the land behind it. I have always wanted to see Spain."

"Are you suggesting we should climb it?" the Marquis asked.

"Why not?" Ola enquired. "It would be very good for us to take some exercise after being cooped up in the yacht for so long."

"I admit to missing my riding," the Marquis agreed, "but I think you would find it a hard climb."

Ola did not answer for a moment. She was looking at small tracks up the side of the cliff which she thought must have been made by wild goats.

Then with a smile she exclaimed:

"That is a challenge! And because I always accept one, I am quite prepared to race you to the top and beyond!"

"Nonsense!" the Marquis replied. "It would be far too much for you. If you would like to sit on the sand you can watch me climb some of the way up, then I can inform you what the view is like."

"I am not going to tell you what I think of that suggestion," Ola replied, "because it would be rude, and I have every intention of climbing the cliff. I am wearing sensible slippers, and I think you will find it far more difficult in your Hessian boots."

"They may certainly prove a handicap," the Marquis replied, "but let me assure you that I am extremely sure-footed, and if you faint by the way-side, or rather on the cliffside, I shall be quite prepared to carry you down."

"You insult me!" Ola cried.

She put down her sunshade as she spoke and looked at the cliff to find where the best place was to start climbing.

She had worn no bonnet all the time she was on the yacht, for the simple reason that she had only the one she had travelled in, and when she sat on deck she either wore a chiffon scarf over her hair or, if it was very sunny, held up a small sunshade.

She did not, however, have to take much trouble over her skin because, as the Marquis had already noted, it had a magnolia-like quality that was the prerogative of some women with red hair and yet even so it was very rare.

It did not brown in the sun, and although she had been out on deck in wind, rain, and sunshine, it still had its dazzling whiteness which was in such direct contrast to the fiery hue of her hair.

The Marquis could understand only too well why women would not only envy her but also dislike her because it would be impossible for her not to draw the eye of every man present, wherever she might be.

It would be simple to dismiss her as looking theatrical, but that was a very superficial view of her looks, which were far more subtle than that.

She had, the Marquis thought, the same

colouring and the same almost spiritual beauty he had seen in a painting but he could not remember where.

Suddenly he knew where he had seen the colour of her hair before — in a picture he himself owned.

By Rubens, it was a portrait of Marchesa Brigida Spinola-Doria. He had always thought not only that it was lovely but also that the gleaming red curls of her hair would be soft and silky to touch and at the same time would have a springing vitality.

He was sure that that was what Ola's hair would feel like.

Then he told himself severely that he had never admired women who were not fair and blue-eyed like Sarah.

Strangely enough, when he thought of her now there was no longer that stabbing pain in his heart, nor was there a red mist before his eyes, and his hands no longer clenched as if he wished to hit somebody.

He felt instead that Sarah, like England, was far away, and when Ola was talking to him so interestingly, drawing him out on his favourite subjects and listening with a rapt expression in her eyes which told him that she was genuinely entranced by what he was saying, Sarah no longer mattered.

Her power to hurt him had gone, and so

too had her power to make him feel that he was a fool to have been betrayed.

He told himself firmly that he still distrusted and disliked all women and would never put himself in the same position again.

At the same time, when the sun was shining and the yacht he had designed himself was showing how remarkably easy she was to handle, there was no point in worrying over what was done and finished with.

Now he was amused by Ola's insistence that they must climb the cliff, as he was quite certain that she would find it too much for her.

They both started, with only a few feet between them, to scramble up the rough rocks and onto the tiny twisting paths which led them higher and higher.

The Marquis was remarkably fit, owing not only to the fact that whenever he was in London or in the country he rode one of his spirited horses every morning.

Although he had not bothered to mention it to Ola, he was an experienced pugilist and sparred in the Gymnasium which was patronised by a great number of his friends.

He was also a swordsman, and although duelling with pistols was far more fashionable, fencing was still a skill in which the Marquis excelled.

Altogether he was extremely proud of being so strong and had no intention of becoming flabby through drink and debauchery like many of the Bucks under the last Monarch.

The King had certainly changed the fashion for large meals which had been set by George IV.

He had just saved fourteen thousand pounds a year by dismissing his brother's German Band and replacing it with a British one — a patriotic but less skilful substitute.

He had then sacked the squadron of French Chefs who had followed the previous King from residence to residence.

This was an economy which was deplored by a number of those who were habitually at the Royal table.

"I find it detestable and depressing," one Statesman had said to the Marquis; while Lord Dudley, who was celebrated for grumbling *sotto-voce* and caused a lot of embarrassment in doing so, had remarked:

"What a change, to be sure! Cold pâtés and hot champagne!"

But while the late King's habitual companions suffered, the public were delighted that William IV had dispensed with the luxurious extravagances of his brother's way of life.

They cheered when they learnt that the number of Royal yachts had been cut from five to two, the stud reduced to half its original size, and that one hundred exotic birds and beasts which had been the delight of George IV were presented to the Zoological Society.

The King was applauded wherever he went, and actually there were few people, if they were honest, who did not admit that a change was overdue.

As the Marquis climbed steadily up the cliff he told himself that for the moment it was a relief to be away from London, free from all the complaints and criticisms which inevitably were voiced amongst those who found the King different in every way from the late Monarch.

For one thing, the Marquis, who was extremely diplomatic when he was acting in an official capacity, found King William's indiscretions dangerous.

He had winced with the Ministers when William had referred to the King of the French as "an infamous scoundrel!"

The Duke of Wellington had given the King a stiff rebuke which had kept him quiet for some weeks, but actually he was irrepressible; and another time, angry at the conduct of affairs by the French, he had startled a Military Banquet at Windsor Castle by expressing the hope that if his guests had to draw their swords, it would be against the French, the natural enemies of England!

"I deserve a holiday," the Marquis said to himself, remembering how he had had to smooth down the incensed feelings of the French Ambassador.

Then he realised that, deep in his thoughts, he had not noticed that Ola was ahead of him.

He told himself she would soon grow tired, but at the same time he moved a little quicker to get level with her.

"Be careful," he admonished. "If you slip you will fall a long way and doubtless end up with a cracked head and a broken leg."

She managed a little smile.

"Stop croaking at me," she said. "I am as sure-footed as any chamois, which, by the way, is an animal I would like to see."

"They are more likely to be found farther inland," the Marquis replied.

"You have visited Spain?"

"I have been to Madrid and Seville."

"How lucky you are! I was just thinking as I was climbing that if I were a man I would be an explorer. What is the point of sitting in one place when one might be travelling all over the world, finding fascinating places where no white man has ever been before?"

"That would certainly be no life for a woman!" the Marquis said.

"I thought that would be your answer," Ola remarked in disgust.

She looked at him, then moved towards the cliff-top so quickly that he had to make a very strenuous effort to catch up with her.

Then suddenly there was a flat rock and as they reached it at almost the same time, Ola gave a little exclamation.

"Look!" she cried. "Caves! How exciting!"

The Marquis stepped onto the flat rock, aware that he was breathing quickly from the exertion and the climb, which had certainly exercised every one of his muscles.

It astounded him to see that Ola was completely composed and the only outward sign of her exertion was that her gown was stained by the moss and lichen that grew on the rocks.

She was looking wide-eyed at the caves behind them, large, dark openings. Then, almost as if with an effort, she turned round to look out to sea.

Below them, and it was a long way down,

they could see the yacht riding at anchor and the men carrying a water-butt, which they had filled at the spring, back towards the boat.

Then beyond was a vista of sparkling blue sea which, in the sunshine, seemed to shimmer with light to where in the indefinable distance the horizon met the sky.

"It is lovely! Absolutely lovely!" Ola exclaimed.

"I agree with you . . ." the Marquis began.

"I wonder . . ." Ola said.

Then she gave a little cry that was stifled as suddenly a rough hand was placed over her mouth and she was lifted off her feet.

She found herself being carried away into the darkness of a cave.

For a moment she could not think what was happening. Then as she struggled and realised that the hands that held her were strong, and that there were four of them, she knew any resistance was useless and could only wonder desperately to where she was being taken.

She had not long to wait, since the dark passage down which she was carried opened suddenly into what was a large cavern lit by flaring torches, with a wood-fire at the far end of it.

Now she was set down on the ground, but

she was still unable to speak because the hand was kept across her mouth.

But she could see, and she saw that standing in the centre of the cave was a man who looked so exactly like the popular conception of a Brigand that it was difficult to believe that he was in fact real.

He had long, dark, greasy hair, a moustache which turned down at the sides of his mouth, and he wore a brightly coloured handkerchief round his head.

In a wide red belt which encircled his waist were knives with ornamented handles, and in his hand he held an old-fashioned pistol.

Standing round the cave were a number of other men dressed like him, the only difference being that the majority of them held knives in their hands instead of a pistol.

The Marquis had obviously put up a fight, for Ola had been in the cave for a few seconds before he was dragged in by three men.

A fourth man was concerned only with keeping his hand over the Marquis's mouth so that he could not speak, and Ola realised that the Brigands were afraid that if he shouted, even though they were so high up, he might alert the attention of the sailors.

The Marquis, seeing the Chief Brigand with his loaded pistol, realised that it was useless to fight any further and he stood still, although his captors kept a firm grip on his arms, and now the man standing behind him covered his mouth with both his hands.

The Brigand Chief merely looked the Marquis up and down, then glanced at Ola.

"What are you waiting for?" one of the men asked. "Kill him and let me have his boots!"

"I could do with his coat," another jeered, "and I bet there's some gold in his pockets!"

The Chief cocked his pistol and Ola saw an expression of delight in his followers' eyes as they bent forward, obviously excited at the thought of seeing a man die.

She could not believe this was happening, but the Brigand Chief had raised his pistol and she knew that he was in fact going to shoot the Marquis, just as he stood there, in cold blood.

Frantically, she bit hard into the hand which covered her mouth, taking her captor by surprise.

He had been far too intent on watching what his Chief was doing to be concerned with her, and when he took his hand away she started to speak.

"No, no, *Señor*, listen a minute!" she shouted in Spanish.

As her voice rang out in the cave the

Brigand Chief looked at her in surprise.

"You must hear what I have to say," Ola went on, "because, *Señor,* if you shoot this nobleman without listening to me first, you will make a very great mistake because you will lose a great deal of money."

She spoke slowly although it was difficult for her because she wanted to scream at the Brigands.

But she realised when they spoke that their Spanish was not the pure Castilian language she had learnt and that they might in fact find her hard to understand.

Then she thought, and she was not mistaken, that the Brigand Chief was better educated and doubtless better bred than his followers.

"So you speak our language, *Señora?*" he said. "What is this man to you — your husband?"

"That is not important," Ola replied. "What you should know is that he is very rich. You do not want his boots, nor his coat. You want the gold he has aboard his ship, which can make you rich for the rest of your lives."

The Brigand Chief and the rest of the party were listening to her almost as if they were spellbound. Then the Chief laughed.

"You paint a very pretty picture, *Señora,*"

he said. "And how do you suggest we collect the gold? Ask the seamen to hand it over?"

"They would be prepared to do so in exchange for their Master's life!"

"We are more likely to receive a bullet in the gullet, *Señora*," the Brigand answered. "No, no, your idea is impracticable. I have seen ships here before, but it is the first time anyone travelling in them was fool enough to trespass on what is my property."

"In which case we can only apologise, *Señor*," Ola said, "and I assure you that if this nobleman gives you his word of honour he will reward you for taking us back in safety to his yacht."

As she spoke the Brigand was looking at her sceptically, and she added:

"Surely I do not have to explain to a Spaniard that no *nobleza* would break his word of honour, as you would not break yours?"

"You are very eloquent, *Señora*," the Brigand Chief said, "but my men do not want money. They are not hungry, as there is plenty of wild game in this part of the country, and if we fancy a fat sheep or a succulent pig for dinner the farmers are too frightened to prevent us from taking them!"

He gave a supercilious smile as he went on:

"No, *Señora,* what my men hanker after

are fashionable boots, a coat that will keep out the rain, and perhaps some pretty jewels that a man can wear in his ears or on his fingers."

"Those I can definitely promise you," Ola said quickly. "I have jewels — diamonds, sapphires, pearls. They are there in the yacht and if you take me back I will give them to you."

There was silence, and she hoped she had made some impression on the Brigand, and yet she was not sure.

He had certainly listened to her and was looking at her now as if he was considering her proposition but could not make up his mind whether to accept or refuse it.

One of his followers rose from where he had been sitting and went up to him to whisper in his ear.

Ola wished she could hear what he was saying, but it was impossible.

The Chief nodded his head, then shook it as if he said "No," and then nodded again.

Ola looked at the Marquis and thought that if perhaps he was looking at her and their eyes met, she would know if he approved or disapproved of what she was trying to do.

But he was watching the two men whispering together in the centre of the cave, and now Ola felt her heart beating apprehensively and was aware that the position they were in was a critical one.

There were several men in the cave and she thought they were more ferocious and in a way more terrifying than any creature she could have imagined in her wildest dreams.

She was sure that they terrorised the countryside and that murder to them was as commonplace as killing the food they wanted to eat.

She found herself remembering the stories she had been told of the bands of ruffians who preyed on travellers all over Europe, to which she had paid little attention.

The girls at the Convent had told her how their relatives or friends had been held up by robbers even on the main highways and to save their lives they had been forced to hand over everything of value they possessed.

But these Brigands seemed to be different.

She could understand, if they lived in a cave like this, that money would not mean a great deal to them.

It was perhaps the excitement of living wild, beholden to no-one, outside the law, that was more attractive than possessions.

Frantically she began to think that her

offer of what they could have in exchange for the Marquis's life was not forceful enough, and she said urgently:

"*Señor,* I have another idea!"

The Chief had been in the process of shaking his head at something his follower had suggested and now he looked at her and said:

"What is it?"

"Suppose one of us, either this nobleman or myself, goes back to the yacht to collect anything you want, clothes, food, boots, gold, jewels. We will put everything on the beach where you can see it quite clearly, and then when your second prisoner is released we can . . . sail . . . away. . . ."

Her voice faltered as if she felt she had not convinced him, and she added:

"What have you to lose by such a suggestion? You could not be identified, nobody could shoot at you, and you would have everything you want."

She thought, although she was not certain, that there was a murmur of approval from some of the other men listening.

The Chief said sharply:

"It is too complicated, and anyway why should we trust you? We have you here and the man shall die, but you will stay with us."

For a moment Ola did not understand

what he meant. Then with an unpleasant smile on his lips he said:

"We have no women with us at the moment and some of my men find you attractive, *Señora.*"

Ola gave a little cry of sheer horror.

"No! No! Do you really think I would . . . stay with you?"

"You have no choice," the Brigand said.

As he spoke he lifted his pistol again, and Ola, with a sudden strength which took them by surprise, fought herself free of her captors and rushed towards the Marquis.

She flung herself in front of him, facing the Brigand and crying as she did so:

"If you shoot him, you will have to shoot me first! You are murderers and the curse of God will strike you sooner or later!"

The words sounded more impressive in Spanish than in English and there was a cry of protest from the Brigand's followers.

At that moment the Marquis struggled wildly with his captors and managed in doing so to release his mouth from the restriction of the hands that had held him.

"Curse you! Yes, curse you!" he shouted, speaking, to Ola's surprise, in Spanish.

Then he was engaged in resisting the men who were struggling to regain their hold on him, while Ola stood between him and the

Chief with his loaded pistol.

She knew that if she moved he would fire it. Then, glancing back at the struggle going on behind her, she saw that one of the Brigands had drawn a knife from his belt and had raised it high to strike the Marquis in the chest.

Without thinking, without even considering what she was doing, Ola threw herself at his arm, forcing the long, sharp, evil-looking blade upwards.

Then as she knew she had not the strength to prevent the Marquis from dying, there was a sudden explosion which seemed so loud as almost to break her ear-drums.

At the same moment she felt the knife pierce her own shoulder, searing its way into her flesh.

As she fell to the ground there were more explosions and the noise of them seemed to bring a darkness that covered her completely. . . .

The Marquis quietly opened the door of the cabin and walked towards the bed, and Gibson, who had been sitting in a chair beside it, rose to his feet.

"How is she?" the Marquis asked in a low voice.

"Running a high fever, M'Lord, and

hasn't regained consciousness, which is what's to be expected."

"I thought I heard her voice during the night," the Marquis said.

"She was delirious, M'Lord, and I didn't know what she were saying."

"I will stay with her now," the Marquis said. "You go and rest, Gibson, and that is an order!"

"Thank you, M'Lord, but I'm all right. I'm used to doing with very little sleep."

"You will be watching over Miss Milford tonight, unless you allow me to do so," the Marquis replied.

"I'll stay with her, M'Lord, as we arranged. But if you'll stay with the young lady now, I'll do as you tells me and have a bit of 'shut-eye.'"

"Do that," the Marquis said. "If she is thirsty, is there anything for her to drink?"

"Yes, M'Lord. There's lime-juice in one jug and fresh water in another."

"The water which nearly cost us dear!" the Marquis remarked as if he were speaking to himself.

Gibson did not reply.

He only gave a last look at Ola to see if there was anything more he could do, then went from the cabin.

The Marquis, left in charge, looked at Ola

and thought that they both were extremely fortunate to be alive. He had been sure that there was no hope for either of them.

He was aware now that it was her brave effort in trying to save his life that had allowed time for the sailors to climb the cliff and appear at precisely the right moment to shoot down the Brigand Chief and six of his men before the rest fled.

"I blame myself, M'Lord," the Captain had said when the Marquis had reached the yacht in safety.

They had had great difficulty in getting Ola, who was unconscious, down from the flat rock outside the caves. They had in fact to lower her with ropes, and the Marquis was afraid that any rough movements would make her shoulder bleed more than it was doing already and she might die from loss of blood.

"Why should you blame yourself?" the Marquis asked.

"It never struck me that Your Lordship and the young lady would climb the cliff," the Captain replied, "and when you started I was actually below, making sure that the water-butts when they came on board would not get loose again, however bad a storm we might encounter."

The Marquis looked as if he approved, and the Captain went on:

"Then when I saw you and Miss Milford climbing upwards, I remembered that the last time I was in this bay I was told to watch out for Spanish Brigands. 'Nasty customers, they are!' one seaman on Lord Lutworth's yacht informed me. 'Cut your throat before they ask your name, and some of 'em are armed with pistols and muskets!'"

"When you remembered this, what did you do?" the Marquis enquired.

"I sent a man up aloft, M'Lord, with a glass, and told him to watch you and the young lady. When he shouted that he could see you being dragged inside the caves, I knew only too well what was happening."

"It was certainly an Act of Providence that your quickness of action saved our lives," the Marquis remarked.

"I'd never have forgiven myself," the Captain said fervently, "if anything had happened to Your Lordship."

"I have been near to death many times in my life," the Marquis replied, "but this was too near for me to wish to encounter such a situation again!"

"I can only thank God that you and Miss Milford returned without worse injuries," the Captain said sincerely.

The Marquis knew that he himself echoed those sentiments.

Now, looking at Ola, he thought it almost impossible to believe that any woman could have been so brave and so resourceful.

He had been surprised to find when he reached the cave that she was not crying or collapsing in the hands of her captors.

Then when she had managed to free her mouth he was aware that she was deliberately speaking slowly in Spanish so that the Brigands could understand what she was saying, and he thought it amazing that she was neither cringing with fear nor pleading.

Then as she stood in front of him to save his life and actually grappled with the Brigand who was trying to knife him, he thought it was an act of heroism he would not have expected from any woman, especially one as young and frail as Ola.

He supposed her fiery red hair reflected the indomitable spirit within her. Certainly only a woman of exceptional bravery could have been involved in so many strange and desperate situations since she had entered his life.

The last was almost incredible, and it was tragic that she, rather than himself, must be the one to suffer what had happened.

The Brigand's knife had gone deep into her shoulder, and by the time they had got her back to the yacht the blood had seeped over her gown in a crimson tide, and her face was so pale that the Marquis was half-afraid that she was in fact dead.

Gibson, who was as skilled as any Surgeon and better than a large number of those the Marquis had known in the Army, took charge in his usual efficient manner.

He and the Marquis had cut Ola's gown off her, to save her from being moved more than was necessary. Then they had cleansed the wound with brandy for fear that the knife had been dirty.

Fortunately, Ola was unconscious when Gibson had stitched the flesh together with such skilled neatness that the Marquis was sure no professional Surgeon could have done better.

The valet had bandaged her deftly and they both knew that the next twenty-four hours would be critical in case the inflammation would be so severe that gangrene would set in.

Gibson had insisted on staying with Ola that night.

"Leave her to me, M'Lord, and you get some rest. Your Lordship can take your turn tomorrow; it's going to be some time before th' lady's on her feet again."

The Marquis had seen the common sense of what his valet said, but although he had gone to bed he found it difficult to sleep while his brain went over and over what had occurred, and his thoughts kept returning to the injured girl in the next cabin.

As he looked at her now, he thought it would be difficult to find anywhere else in the world a face so lovely and at the same time so unusual.

He realised for the first time that her eye-lashes were dark at the tips and shaded away to gold where they touched her skin; similarly, the winged eye-brows above them were dark, while her hair against the white linen pillow was like a flame.

It made him think of the torches flaring in the Brigands' cave, and he wondered if any of the men who had fled in terror when the sailors had killed their comrades would ever go back.

He had the feeling that as their Leader was dead this particular gang of ruffians would be disbanded, and at least a few wretched travellers would escape persecution at their hands in the future.

At the same time, the Marquis told himself it was a salutary lesson that he should have learnt long ago, not to take chances in foreign countries.

There were so many parts of Europe that were wild and uncivilised, and he was aware that even if Ola had travelled on the main highway to Paris she would have been in danger.

She might have been molested, perhaps not by Brigands but certainly by thieves who would relieve her of the jewellery she carried, and by men who would find her looks irresistible and would be equally prepared to use violence to get what they wanted.

"How can any woman take such risks with herself?" the Marquis asked himself angrily.

Then he realised that he had forgotten how young, innocent, and inexperienced Ola was.

Since they had been talking to each other on equal terms he had found it hard to remember her age and that she was in some ways, little more than a child.

He found himself remembering how she had puzzled over the word "cocotte" and supposed it referred to some kind of actress.

'Some man will take it upon himself to enlighten her about such things, one of these days,' the Marquis thought cynically. 'Then she will be like every other woman — pursuing men and, having caught one, prepared to manipulate him to suit her own ends.'

Once again he was thinking of Sarah. Then he recalled how Ola had told him that she had no wish to marry and submit to being ordered about by a husband.

'He will be an exceptional man to get his own way,' the Marquis thought with a smile.

A sudden movement caught his attention.

She was moving her head from side to side and now she said in an indistinct murmur:

"I . . . must . . . escape . . . I must! . . . Help . . . me . . . oh . . . help me!"

The Marquis rose and put his hand on her forehead. It was very hot and he knew that her temperature was rising.

She moved again restlessly, and although Gibson had bound her arm tightly to her side, the Marquis was afraid that she might break open the wound.

He went to the basin where Gibson had left a clean linen handkerchief and beside it a bottle of *eau-de-Cologne*.

The Marquis soaked the handkerchief in the Cologne and some water, then squeezed it out, and when it was moist and cool he put it on Ola's forehead as she murmured:

"It is . . . foggy . . . do . . . be careful! . . . Look out!"

He knew she was back in the post-chaise, reliving the difficulties and the drama of her escape from her Stepmother.

"It is all right, Ola," he said gently, "you are safe and you must go to sleep."

She was still for some minutes, as if the handkerchief on her forehead was soothing.

Then with a little cry she said agitatedly:

"I . . . cannot go back . . . I have to . . . escape again . . . I hate him! I . . . hate him! How . . . can I . . . save . . . myself . . . ?"

There was something pathetic in the last words and the Marquis said softly:

"You have saved yourself. Listen to me, Ola, you are safe, and you do not have to go back to your Stepmother — do you understand?"

He was not certain whether his words reached her or not, but he thought, although he was not sure, that some of the tension seemed to go from her body.

Then once again she appeared to fall asleep.

"I suppose I have committed myself now," the Marquis told himself ruefully. "Whether she heard me or not, I have told her she will not return to her Stepmother, and that is a promise I have to keep!"

CHAPTER SIX

"I congratulate you, young lady, on having been lucky enough to have your wound treated so expertly," the Doctor said.

He was a hearty man who had been summoned on board at Gibraltar to examine Ola's wound, and he could in fact find nothing wrong with it.

"I expect you're feeling exhausted after your fever," he went on, "but with rest and good food you'll soon be on your feet again."

"What about a tonic?" the Marquis suggested, who had come into the cabin after the Doctor had finished examining Ola.

The Doctor glanced round the luxurious surroundings and said with a twinkle in his eye:

"The best tonic I can prescribe comes from France."

The Marquis smiled.

"I presume you mean champagne?"

"It's what I always prescribe for my richer patients," the Doctor said, "but the poorer ones expect a bottle from me, which is usually little more than coloured water!"

The Marquis laughed.

"At least you are frank."

"I believe it's a patient's will-power that counts," the Doctor said. "If they want to get well, they get well; if they want to die, they die!"

The Marquis noted that Ola, weak though she was, was smiling at this exchange of words and now she gave a little chuckle.

"I come into the first category," she said, "and I want to live."

"Then as I've already said, we shall soon have you up and dancing," the Doctor answered.

He glanced at Ola's hair before he left the cabin, and she heard him say outside the door:

"It's seldom I have the privilege of attending so beautiful a young lady!"

Ola listened for the Marquis's reply but they had moved too far away, and she wondered if he had qualified the Doctor's compliment by complaining that she was also a nuisance, a positive encumbrance.

When she had regained consciousness she had learnt how much trouble she had given.

It was Gibson who had told her that the Marquis had sat with her every day when she was delirious and running too high a fever to be left alone.

'He must have been terribly bored,' she thought.

Then she told herself that she had upset him in so many different ways that one more would make little difference.

But when she was on the way to recovery, she realised that the Marquis was sitting with her when there was really no need for him to do so.

He read to her and was not offended when she fell asleep, and as soon as she could sit up in bed they played chess and piquet and, what she enjoyed more than anything else, they talked.

It was after they had left Gibraltar and were moving over the blue sea of the Mediterranean that Ola began to feel more like her former self.

Gibson was sure that it was due not to the champagne but to the fresh oranges and lemons he had been able to buy in Gibraltar.

"I've seen too many sailors, Miss, suffer from lack of fruit when they were a long time at sea," he said, "not to realise how important it is, especially when there's a wound that needs healing."

Because Ola was prepared to believe that he was right, she drank glass after glass of the juices he prepared for her, and she had to admit that they seemed to speed the healing of her wound.

"Will I have a scar?" she asked Gibson when he was dressing it.

"I'll tell you no lie, Miss," he replied. "You'll carry a mark there to your dying day, but fortunately it's not in a place where it'll show unless your evening-gowns are cut over-low."

Ola laughed.

"I must remember to make them discreetly modest."

When she told the Marquis what Gibson had said, he laughed too.

"You will certainly not be expected when you go to Court to have a very low décolletage," he said, "not with Queen Adelaide's eye upon you."

He spoke without thinking, and only as he saw Ola blush did he remember that if her behaviour at this moment were known in Society, she would receive no invitation to Buckingham Palace and would be ostracised by all the important hostesses of the Social World.

He thought with a frown that that must not happen, and he decided that before they reached Nice he must find some solution to Ola's problems. Above all, she must have a Chaperone.

As if she knew what he was thinking but felt too tired to argue about it at the moment, Ola shut her eyes.

He thought she was asleep and after some minutes he very quietly left her cabin. Then she lay staring at the ceiling and wondering once again despairingly what would happen to her in the future.

After four days' sailing in the Mediterranean, Ola was well enough to be carried up on deck.

"What you wants Miss, is some good fresh air, to put the colour back in your cheeks," Gibson said.

Ola thought he sounded exactly like her old Nurse, who had always believed that fresh air was a cure for everything, including a bad temper.

When she was on deck she realised why the Marquis looked so well and did not seem to mind that they were sailing more slowly towards Nice than they would have done if she had not been on board.

Although the sunshine was warm the sea was cold, but he swam in it twice a day, once in the morning and again in the afternoon.

She liked to watch him swimming until his head was only a little spot in the distance, but she would feel anxious in case anything should happen which would prevent him from returning to the yacht in safety.

She found herself remembering the stories of men who had cramps in the sea and sank before anyone could rescue them.

When she enquired about sharks she was told that there were none in this area and the only thing the Marquis had to be afraid of was catching a chill.

"He's unlikely to do that," Gibson said, and added with pride in his voice: "There's few men as strong as His Lordship, and whether he's riding or hunting it's always the horse as tires before His Lordship."

Ola found that when he was not swimming the Marquis liked to take the helm of the yacht and sail the *Sea Wolf* himself.

She realised how expert he was and that he could sail closer to the wind than anyone else aboard without letting the sails flap.

She thought it must give him the same thrill as driving his Phaeton to break a record or riding his own horse past the winning-post in a steeple-chase.

Lying comfortably on the soft couch which Gibson had constructed for her on deck, and propped against silk cushions, Ola found the activities going on all round her far more fascinating than being alone in her cabin.

She was taken down below when the sun began to sink, and, as often happened, a chill wind blew up and the Marquis usually came with her.

Then they would talk and to Ola's delight they would discuss subjects as diverse as Oriental religions and the Abolition of the Slave Trade.

The Marquis was astounded not only at the subjects which interested her but because she knew so much about them.

"How can you have read so much at your age?" he asked one evening after they had had a long and animated discussion on the conditions in the coal-mines.

"I have not only read a lot," Ola replied, "but Papa was an extremely clever man. The only trouble was that he wished to expound his own theories and not listen to anybody else's."

The Marquis smiled.

"So that is why you are so verbose on these subjects."

"That is a rather unkind way of putting it," Ola objected, "but the answer is 'yes.' I have been bottling up my own ideas for so long that now, because you are obliging enough to listen to me, they burst out like a volcano."

The Marquis laughed and thought that while he was the first man Ola had ever been able to talk to, she was the first woman who had ever been interested in every subject in the world except himself.

He had never before in his life, the Marquis thought, talked for hours with a woman, and an attractive one at that, when there had been nothing personal in what they said to each other.

With Ola there were no flirtatious glances, no fishing for compliments, and, most of all, none of the sharp, witty *double entendres* which the sophisticated women in London used as a weapon of attraction.

Thinking back, he could not remember ever having a conversation with Sarah which had not involved her feelings or his, and which had not ended in his making passionate expressions of his love for her.

He realised now how cleverly she had led him on, how she had aroused, then tantalised him by refusing to "risk her reputation" by surrendering herself as he wished her to do.

Yet all the time she was amusing herself with another man.

To his surprise, he found that his hurt pride as well as his anger had now subsided to the point where he could wonder quite calmly what Sarah must have thought when he did not arrive the following night as she had expected.

He imagined that she would have waited for him, then must have decided that he could not have received her letter.

She would therefore have expected him the next day and perhaps the day after that, until finally she would either have made enquiries or somebody would have told her that he had stayed one night at Elvin and then had left at dawn the following morning.

It was then, he thought, unless she was more stupid than he gave her credit for being, that she would have realised what had happened and been aware that she had lost him irretrievably.

"I hope she is upset," he told himself, and found that he was not even feeling very vindictive about it.

She had gambled and lost, as many men and women had done in the past and would do in the future.

For the first time the Marquis said to himself:

"Thank God I was lucky enough to find out the truth before it was too late!"

He had had a lucky escape and he knew he should be grateful for that, just as he was grateful that Ola had saved his life when, if she had not been there, he would undoubtedly have died at the hands of the Brigands.

Several days before they reached Nice, Ola was able to go up on deck without being carried, and she was well enough not only to have luncheon with the Marquis in the Saloon but also to stay up for dinner.

"I have been given strict instructions by Gibson that I am to go to bed before you drink your first glass of port," she said, "so please do not be in a hurry to do so."

"You know Gibson has to be obeyed when it is a question of your health," the Marquis said with mock seriousness.

"I am well aware of that," Ola replied. "He gets more like my Nurse every day until I find myself almost saying: 'Yes, Nanny!' and 'No, Nanny!' to everything he tells me to do."

The Marquis laughed and she added quickly:

"But I am not complaining! I realise that if Gibson had not been on board I might not be here with you now."

"He is really rather a wonderful little man."

"He thinks the sun and the moon rise and set for you," Ola said. "He sings your praises until I too bow to your importance."

"You are trying to make me feel embarrassed," the Marquis complained, "and I suspect there is a sting somewhere in what you are saying."

"Now you are being nasty," Ola teased. "You are omnipotent and I feel that by the end of this voyage I shall be saying my prayers to you."

She spoke without considering her words.

Then as the Marquis saw a sudden wary look in her eyes and the colour rise in her cheeks, he knew she was thinking that if she was praying to him, it would be to beg him not to send her back to her Stepmother, which he could quite easily do from Nice.

He hesitated, as if he intended to say something, but before he could do so the steward came into the Saloon and the opportunity did not seem to arise later.

The *Sea Wolf* sailed into the Harbour at Nice early in the morning, and Ola could see the white Villas and Hotels built along the sea-front and above them the surrounding hills, and silhouetted against the sky in the far distance the snow-capped, rugged head of Mont Chauve.

Everything seemed to glow with a warmth and radiance which made her feel as if Nice gave her a special welcome, and before they dropped anchor she could see the palms, the graceful feathery tamarisks, the oleanders, and, what she longed for more than anything else, the yellow mimosas.

"I want to go ashore immediately!" she cried excitedly to the Marquis.

Then as he did not reply she looked up at him and saw a frown between his eyes.

"You think that would be . . . unwise?" she asked quickly.

"What I would like to do," he replied, "is to have a quick look round to see whom I know here. This, as you are well aware, is a fashionable time of the year for people to come to Nice, and I would not wish you to be embarrassed until we have made our plans."

"Yes . . . of course," Ola said quickly.

She realised now that they should have discussed what she was to do before they had actually arrived.

But she had been content to let the days drift by without forcing the issue, and she had the idea that the Marquis was being kind to her because she was still weak from her wound.

"I am sure you are right," she said. "You must go ashore, and I will wait until you return."

He smiled as if he thought she was being not only sensible but conciliatory in a way he had not expected.

"I shall not be long," he said. "I know where to make enquiries and I shall come back as quickly as possible."

"I will sit and look at the view," she said. "It is so lovely — like a picture by a master-painter of which one would never grow tired."

The Marquis left the yacht and Ola thought he looked extremely elegant with his top-hat at an angle on his dark head.

She wondered if there were many of his old loves staying in Nice who would welcome him with open arms.

She hoped that if they did so it would not make him linger for long, because without him the yacht seemed empty and she felt lonely.

After a while she went down to the Saloon and, choosing a book, settled herself down to read.

It was full of interesting things she thought she would like to discuss with the Marquis, and yet she kept wondering if, now that they had reached Nice, this would be the end of the voyage as far as she was concerned.

She could hardly believe that he would be so cruel or so heartless after what had happened to send her back to her Stepmother as he had threatened to do before she had drugged him.

But what was the alternative? Unless she

went, as she had first intended, to the Convent and risked her cousin Giles finding her there.

It struck her that she had not thought about Giles since the moment she had left Dover with the Marquis, and she supposed that he would have been well looked after wherever he was staying.

If he was not, it could hardly be her fault. He had no right to behave as he had or to threaten that he would force her into marriage just so that he could possess her fortune.

"He is horrible and I have no wish to think about him!" Ola told herself.

She was quite certain that the Marquis would never behave in such an ungentlemanly manner however much in need he might be of money.

Besides, she was sure that, unlike Giles, in straitened circumstances the Marquis would be clever enough to find some way of making money and would not just sponge on his friends or relations.

'He would be too honourable,' Ola thought.

She had picked up her book to go on reading, when she heard footsteps outside the Saloon and thought with a leap of her heart that the Marquis had returned.

She looked eagerly towards the door as it

opened and a steward appeared to say:

"A gentleman to see His Lordship!"

Then a man walked into the Saloon and as Ola stared at him incredulously she realised with astonishment that it was Giles.

After his first start at seeing her, he said harshly:

"So this is where you are! I might have suspected it when I was told that the Marquis of Elvington had taken you across the Channel to Calais."

"Why . . . are you . . . here?"

"I was looking for you," Giles replied, "although I did not expect to find you in Nice!"

She did not speak, and as if he thought he must explain himself he said:

"When I was well enough to travel, I went to the Convent, expecting to find you there."

That was what Ola had guessed he would do, and she drew in her breath as he continued:

"I was not certain where I should go next, and I came to Nice to convalesce after my accident. You have not asked after my health and it may interest you to know that I fractured two ribs and my head still aches."

"You got what you deserve," Ola replied sharply, "and I was lucky to escape from you!"

"To the Marquis of Elvington!"

There was no doubt from the way Giles spoke that he was sneering, and Ola said:

"His Lordship was kind enough to help me when you were trying to force me into marriage just so that you could get your hands on my fortune."

"I was at least prepared to marry you," Giles sneered, "but I always thought that with your hair you would become a strumpet sooner or later!"

He spoke so aggressively that he was not aware, as Ola was, that the Marquis had come into the Saloon behind him.

Now as he finished speaking he turned his head and saw who was there.

"You will kindly apologise for speaking to your cousin in such a manner!" the Marquis said quietly.

"I shall do no such thing!" Giles retorted. "I called her a strumpet, which she obviously is, but because we are related I am still prepared to make an honest woman of her, which is more than you are prepared to do."

He spat the words at the Marquis, then as Ola gasped the Marquis knocked him down.

It was a blow to the chin, and as Giles sprawled on the deck of the Saloon the Marquis said:

"Get off my yacht! If I ever find you here

again, or speaking in such an insulting way to a woman, I will give you the thrashing you deserve!"

For a moment Giles did not move, and Ola thought the expression on his face was so unpleasant that it was positively evil.

Then as he picked himself up he said:

"If you think you can get away with this, Elvington, you are very much mistaken! When I get back to London I shall make it my business to see that everybody in the Social World is aware of your behaviour in abducting a young and defenceless girl. I cannot believe His Majesty or the Queen will countenance such immorality on the part of one of their privileged entourage."

As he finished speaking Ola gave a little cry of horror, then as Giles walked from the cabin, stroking his chin where he had been hit, and the Marquis following him, she ran to her own cabin.

She knew that Giles had not spoken idly in saying that the Marquis would be in disgrace if the King and Queen heard his distorted version of her being alone and unchaperoned on the Marquis's yacht.

The Queen had been generous enough to accept the burden of His Majesty's illegitimate children and to become devoted to them, but in every other way she had shown herself to be prudish and extremely censorious about anything that offended her particular ideals of morality and respectability.

Having been brought up in a narrow and provincial Court, she had a very clear vision of what conventional life should be and had no idea of modifying her beliefs to suit an alien land.

Ola was intelligent enough to realise that the Marquis was not only proud of the confidence placed in him by the King but also made it his duty to try to prevent the Monarch from making the many mistakes in which his impetuosity involved him.

She had also learnt quite casually in their conversations that when people at Court and even the Prime Minister wanted something done, they asked the Marquis to help put their point of view to the King simply because His Majesty was so fond of him.

"How can I take that from him? How can I spoil that part of his life?" Ola asked herself.

Because she could think of nothing else she could do, she frantically began to pack her trunk, taking her gowns from the cupboard in which they hung and her other things from the drawers which were in a cleverly contrived piece of furniture which fitted against the side of one of the walls of the cabin.

Because she was agitated it took her longer than it would have done normally, apart from the fact that because she was using her injured arm it began to hurt her.

But at last everything was packed, and she took her bonnet from the top of the cupboard, put it on her head, and tied the ribbons under her chin.

Then she went to the cabin door and called for a steward.

There was always one in attendance when she and the Marquis were in their cabins, but it was not the steward who came in answer to her call; it was Gibson.

"I wanted the steward," she said.

"I'll do whatever it is you want, Miss."

Ola hesitated a moment, then she said:

"Please have my trunk strapped down and taken onto the Quay, and I want a hackney-carriage."

Gibson did not reply and after a moment she said firmly:

"At once!"

"I'm afraid that's impossible, Miss."

"What do you mean . . . it is impossible?" Ola enquired.

"Before the Master went ashore, Miss, he says to me: 'Look after Miss Milford, Gibson, until I gets back.' "

"What His Lordship said or did not say

does not concern me," Ola said with dignity. "I have to leave, Gibson, and I would be obliged if you would carry out my orders."

"I'm sorry, Miss, but that's something I can't do!"

"You mean you are refusing to have my trunk taken ashore?"

"If it comes to that, Miss, I'm refusing to let you go," Gibson answered. "Besides, you're not strong enough to go gallivanting about, and you knows that as well as I do."

"I . . . have to . . . go, Gibson."

He shook his head; and then instead of raging at him as she was sure she would have done in the past, she sat down helplessly on the bed.

"Now, what I'm going to do, Miss," Gibson said in a different tone, "is to fetch you a nice cup of tea. There's nothing like a cup of tea when you feels upset."

He went from the cabin as he spoke, shutting the door behind him, and Ola put her hands up to her eyes as if in an effort to think.

"If I stay here I shall hurt the Marquis," she said, "and that is something I must not do."

She decided that if Gibson was going to be so obstructive she must leave without her luggage.

She knew he would have gone to the galley to make her tea, and she thought that if she hurried she could slip up on deck and get away before he was aware of it.

The *Sea Wolf* was tied up alongside the Quay and there was a gangplank by which she could step ashore.

She therefore picked up her jewel-case, and, moving very quietly in case there was anyone listening, she went to the door and turned the handle.

It seemed surprisingly stiff, and then as she turned it again she realised indignantly that Gibson had locked her in!

It was intolerable behaviour on his part, and she walked to the port-hole, wishing that she were small enough to squeeze through it and swim to the shore, just to show her independence.

Then she knew that that was impossible and once again she sat down on her bed, and taking off her bonnet she threw it down in a display of temper, which, however, only made her feel more tired than she was already.

Then she heard Gibson returning and thought she would tell him in no uncertain terms what she thought of his impertinence in daring to treat her as if she were a child.

He had been so kind and skilful when she

was ill, but now he was exceeding his authority.

She heard the key turn in the lock and then the door opened, but it was not Gibson who stood there but the Marquis.

He came into the cabin and she saw him glance at her packed trunk and thought he already knew what she was trying to do.

Then as his eyes met hers, she found that her words of protest died on her lips. She could only look at him and think how handsome he was and how strong he had appeared when he had knocked Giles down.

"I am sorry to have been so long," the Marquis said. "You must have been wondering where I had gone."

"I . . . I wanted to . . . leave . . . but Gibson would not let me."

"Where were you going?"

"Away . . . so that Giles cannot . . . hurt you by the things he would tell the . . . King and Queen."

"I think your leaving in such a precipitate manner would hardly alter his story if he was permitted to tell it."

Ola's eyes widened.

"You stopped him from doing so?"

The Marquis nodded.

"But . . . how? What have you . . . done?"

It flashed through Ola's mind that the

Marquis had injured Giles or even killed him. Then she knew that that would mean he would be in worse trouble than he was already. Besides, it seemed somehow out-of-character.

She was still sitting on the bed, and now the Marquis walked to the end of it to lean his arms on the ornate brass end, where he stood looking at her.

Unexpectedly Ola found herself apologising.

"I am so sorry," she said, "I did not think when I . . . forced you to bring me away from England . . . that I could hurt you . . . and now . . . after what Giles has said . . . I realise what I have . . . done, and I can only say how . . . very . . . very sorry I am."

"Because you have said that," the Marquis answered, "it makes it easier for me to tell you how I have contrived that Giles will not be able to damage either of us with the tale he wished to relate in London, and he would undoubtedly have done so had I not prevented it."

"What have you done? You must tell me!" Ola said.

"I told your cousin," the Marquis said, "that we are married!"

For the moment Ola felt as if she could not have heard him aright. Then as she looked at him, her eyes so wide in her pale face that they seemed to fill it, she saw the confirmation in his and said:

"How could you have said such a thing? When he finds out it is not true it will only make things worse."

"But it is true," the Marquis said quietly. "We are, in fact, already married legally, although I am sure you would like a Church Service. So I have arranged one for this evening."

He saw that Ola was so astonished that she was speechless, and he explained:

"In France one has to be married first in front of the Mayor at the Town Hall, and it is permitted that one of the persons concerned be represented by proxy."

He smiled before he continued:

"The proxy has to be a responsible person and so, as I thought the Captain would qualify in that capacity, I took him with me!"

"Are you really saying . . . that I . . . I am your . . . wife?" Ola asked.

"I have the document to prove it," the Marquis answered, "but as I think every woman is entitled to be present at her own wedding, we will be married very quietly tonight after sunset at the Protestant Church. The Vicar is not only very willing to perform the ceremony but has promised to keep it a secret."

For a moment there was complete silence in the cabin, until Ola said in a frightened little voice:

"B-but . . . you said you . . . hated women and did not want to . . . marry anybody!"

"And you," the Marquis replied, "said you hated men and had no wish to be married."

There was again a long silence. Then he said:

"I feel sure, Ola, you will be sensible and intelligent enough to know that we both have to make the best of a difficult situation that has been brought about through your cousin. It is actually something I should have anticipated, but while you were convalescing I did not wish to trouble you with plans for the future."

"That was . . . kind of you," Ola said, "but this is . . . all my fault . . . and I am . . . ashamed."

"I think any blame you might attach to your action in forcing yourself upon me is certainly fully compensated and erased by the way in which you saved my life."

"I saved you," Ola said, "but you would not have climbed the cliff and gone into . . . danger had I not . . . challenged you to do so."

"You can think that now," the Marquis answered, "but if I had been alone I might easily have climbed for the exercise and the same thing would have happened, only with a far different ending to the story."

He saw that she was not convinced and he added:

"What has happened has happened and there is never any point in looking back in life and saying: 'If I had done that, or something else, it would all have been different.' "

He gave a little laugh before he said:

"Neither of us can rewrite history, but what we can do is to be wise enough not to fight against the inevitable or, as you are very fond of doing, to run away, as that will solve nothing."

"I thought if I . . . left you . . . you would be able to persuade Giles not to . . . tell anybody that I had been on the *Sea Wolf*. I am sure, because he is always short of money, that you could have . . . bribed him to keep silent."

"And have him blackmail me for the rest of my life?" the Marquis enquired. "No, thank you, Ola! I prefer my own solution, and perhaps you will not find it so unpleasant being married to me as it would have been if you had married your cousin or were on your own."

"I . . . thought," Ola said in a low voice, "that when he was lying on the . . . floor he looked really . . . evil . . . and I am sure he will try to . . . hurt you if he can."

"I think we can be sure that he will be unable to do that," the Marquis said. "As I intend to send a notice of our marriage to the *Gazette* immediately, he will find when he reaches England that nobody will listen to anything he has to say."

Ola thought this over for a minute, then she said in a very low voice:

"He called me a . . . strumpet. Is that the same as being a . . . *fille de joie?*"

The Marquis hesitated for only a moment before he answered:

"Yes."

"And 'cocotte' . . . means the . . . same?"

He nodded.

"Now . . . I . . . understand how horrible and insulting my Stepmother was being to me . . . and perhaps . . ."

She paused for a moment before she added:

"P-perhaps your friends will think it . . . very wrong of you to . . . m-marry somebody who looks like . . . me."

The Marquis smiled.

"My friends when they see you, will think I am very lucky to have married somebody who is, beyond all question, extremely beautiful!"

He saw by the expression on her face that Ola did not believe him, and he exclaimed:

"Good Heavens, child, you cannot be unaware that because you are so lovely your Stepmother and, I imagine, many other women you meet are wildly jealous of your looks?"

"Do you . . . mean that?" Ola asked. "I have always felt there is . . . something wrong . . . because people are so surprised at the colour of my hair."

"They are surprised because it is very rare for a woman to have that particular colour and be so beautiful."

He was paying her a compliment, and yet she thought his voice sounded almost indifferent, as if he were discussing an inanimate object rather than a human being.

"I am glad . . . very glad that you need not . . . be ashamed of me," she said after a moment.

"I can promise you I will never be that," the Marquis said. "And now, as there need be no more restrictions on your appearance with me in Nice or anywhere else, I suggest after luncheon I take you for a drive. The views from Villefranche, which is just along the coast road, are very fine."

"I would love that! May I really come with you?"

"I will order luncheon to be served immediately," the Marquis replied.

He went from the cabin and Ola sat down in front of the dressing-table to tidy her hair.

As she stared at her reflection in the mirror she thought of how the Marquis had said that she was beautiful, at the same time with a note in his voice which made her sure that it meant nothing to him personally.

"I want him to think me beautiful," she told herself.

Then she remembered that she was now his wife, and she felt herself shiver because she was afraid that after all he hated her because he had been tricked into marriage, against every inclination to remain a bachelor.

"How could I have known that this would happen?" she asked herself.

She was suddenly ashamed of the fact that she had behaved in such an outrageous way that would make any man dislike her and decide to keep out of her way.

She had drugged him so that for three days he had been unconscious. Then when he could have rid himself of her at Gibraltar or Marseilles, he had been too kind to do so because she had a knife-wound in her shoulder.

And now, to save his reputation and hers, he had been forced to marry her. She could see that it was a conclusive answer to keep Giles's mouth shut, but it was a heavy price to pay.

"He will never forgive me . . . never!" she told herself, and felt something like a physical pain in her heart at the thought.

Then strangely she found herself praying that somehow she could persuade him not to hate her.

She prayed that he would find her, although it was unlikely, the type of wife he wanted, who could talk to him about his ambitions, the work he was doing in the House of Lords, and try to run his houses in the way he wanted them run.

"I will make no demands on him," she told herself.

Then she wondered if that was all a man wanted in marriage. Surely he would want more?

She knew the answer almost as if somebody had said it aloud.

A man would want love; but was that something she could give the Marquis?

She asked the question and saw her own eyes staring back at her, wide and a little frightened.

Then she knew the answer but was afraid to put it into words.

CHAPTER SEVEN

"Forasmuch as Boyden and Ola have consented together in Holy Wedlock and have witnessed the same before God, and thereto have given and pledged their troth each to the other, and have declared the same by the giving and receiving of a ring and by joining of hands, I pronounce that they be man and wife together, in the name of the Father and of the Son, and of the Holy Ghost. Amen."

It was true, Ola thought. She was married to the Marquis!

She had felt ever since leaving the yacht that she was moving in a dream and that everything had such a sense of unreality that she might still be in the fog in which they had first met.

In fact nothing had seemed real since he had told her that they were already married legally and that he had arranged a Church Service in the evening.

Immediately after luncheon, when conversation had been a little difficult, the Marquis had taken her, as he had promised, driving round Nice.

It had been a short drive because after they had seen the view from Villefranche he had ordered the carriage to return to the yacht.

"I want you to rest," he said. "You have been through another dramatic experience today, and nothing is more tiring."

Although she was thrilled by the sunshine, the sea, and the flowers, Ola knew that the way Giles had behaved and the packing she had done herself had left her somewhat exhausted.

When they arrived back on the yacht she had obeyed the Marquis and had gone to her cabin and got into bed.

She had thought she would lie awake thinking about their marriage, but as soon as her head touched the pillows she had fallen asleep.

It had been a deep and dreamless sleep, and she had awakened only when Gibson came to her cabin to insist on looking at her shoulder.

"It is all right," she said quickly.

"I've warned you, Miss, against doing too much," Gibson said sternly, adopting his Nanny role again as he always did when he was tending to her wound.

Because she knew it was hopeless to argue with him, she let him take the light dressing from her shoulder and put on another one.

She suspected that as the wound had healed so well even a dressing was unnecessary, but she had the feeling that Gibson enjoyed nursing her and was determined not to relinquish his authority until the very last moment.

"Now, I think you should get dressed, Miss," Gibson said, "and there's a special gown here for you to wear."

"A gown!" Ola exclaimed in surprise.

"Yes, Miss. His Lordship bought it this afternoon, and as I gives him the exact right measurements, I'd be surprised if it doesn't fit."

Ola was astonished not only at receiving a present of a new gown but because the Marquis had taken so much trouble over her.

She knew, now that she was awake again, that it was impossible for her thoughts not to keep returning to him, remembering that while he had no wish to be married he had been pressured into it through circumstances.

She had been glad that Giles's evil intentions towards them both had been circumvented by their marriage and that the Marquis would not lose his special relationship with the King.

At the same time, it was not his public life

with which she was concerned, and when she thought of how she had forced herself on him when he had wished to be rid of her she felt more and more ashamed.

She was now an encumbrance not only on a voyage but for life!

When Gibson returned to her cabin carrying a gown in his hands she could only think that the Marquis was not only making, as he had said, the best of a situation in which they were both involved, but was actually embellishing it in a way she had not expected.

The gown was lovely and when she put it on she knew that it made her look exactly as a bride should — ethereal, spiritual, and like a fairy-Princess.

The full skirt swept the ground in front and had a train at the back, the bodice tapered to a tiny waist, and the white gauze of which the gown was made was ornamented with silver ribbons caught with orange-blossoms.

It seemed part of the golden mimosa trees she had seen with the Marquis, the shrubs heavy with brilliant flowers, and the shimmering sunlight which gave everything a glittering glow which seemed to come from Heaven itself.

"It fits like a glove, Miss!" Gibson exclaimed.

Ola knew he was delighted not only with her but with himself for having got her measurements right.

He went from the cabin and came back with a wreath of orange-blossoms which matched those on her gown, and with it a lace veil so fine that it might have been made by a spider.

Ola allowed him to arrange it over her red hair and she knew that nothing could be more becoming and that it gave her a look of purity and innocence which every bride should have.

"It's a pity, Miss, that you can't wear one of them tiaras that His Lordship has in the safe at Elvin," Gibson said. "Very fine they are, and there's emeralds which will suit you when you goes to a Ball."

"I am very happy with the orange-blossoms," Ola said in a low voice.

She thought it would be pretentious of her to think that she would ever wear the family jewels that belonged to the Marquis, and she knew that today she had no wish to open her own jewel-case.

Somehow at the back of her mind she had the feeling that because her wedding was so strange and unusual, everything about it should be very simple.

That she looked like a bride was the

choice of the Marquis and she would leave in his hands everything which concerned herself.

In a way it would be an apology to him, she thought, and she wondered if he would understand.

When she was ready she suddenly felt afraid of leaving the cabin and she thought that perhaps when she went into the Saloon she would see a frown between the Marquis's eyes and would know how much he was disliking the ceremony which was awaiting them.

"Perhaps he would like to run away, as I have always run away when things became too difficult," she told herself.

Then she remembered that they were in fact married already, although she was sure that no-one on the yacht knew anything about it except the Captain.

Only because Gibson insisted and because she could think of no reason not to do so, she walked into the Saloon proudly, with her chin up.

As she had expected, the Marquis was there, and when she saw him she was astonished at his appearance because he was wearing evening-dress.

Then she remembered that the girls at the Convent had told her that in France the bridegroom always wore evening-dress whatever time of day the ceremony took place.

But as her wedding was in the evening it actually was entirely appropriate.

He certainly looked magnificent, and looking at him she forgot her own appearance.

She saw that he was not frowning or looking disagreeable but was regarding her with a smile on his lips.

"Thank you," she said hurriedly, "thank you . . . so much for my . . . gown. I did not expect you to think of . . . such things . . . but I am . . . very grateful."

"If you are ready, I suggest we leave for the Church immediately," the Marquis said. "There is a carriage waiting on the Quay. In fact there are two, as the Captain is coming with us as a witness and will be travelling in the second one."

Ola did not reply, she merely followed the Marquis onto the deck and was glad both for the darkness and for the veil over her face, which was a protection from any curious eyes that might be watching her.

However, there appeared to be nobody about, and when she stepped into the closed carriage which was waiting by the gangplank the Marquis joined her and they set off immediately.

She thought she ought to speak to him, but as he did not say anything to her they drove in silence and there were only the lights of the Villas and Hotels lining the road to make her feel as if she were going on a strange voyage to an unknown destination.

The Church, however, was not far away and when they arrived the Marquis got out first to help her alight, then offered her his arm.

It was only a few steps to the porch, then they were inside the Church and by the light of the candles on the altar Ola could see that it was small and had stained-glass windows and stone pillars.

What made it different were the mass of lilies in the chancel and the profusion of white carnations which decorated the base of the pillars and the empty choir-stalls.

It gave the Church a beauty she had not expected and the fragrance of the flowers filled the air almost like incense.

The Marquis took her up the aisle to where the Parson was waiting for them and when they stood in front of him he immediately began the Service.

The Marquis made his responses in a firm voice, but to Ola her own voice sounded so strange that she barely recognised it.

She knew that she was frightened and she felt as if she were making an irretrievable step into the unknown, and yet there was nothing she could do and she felt as if she were being swept along on a tide which carried her into an unknown sea.

When the Parson blessed the ring Ola felt the Marquis's fingers holding her hand and the strength of them seemed to give her courage.

They knelt and she found herself praying that somehow their marriage would be a happy one and that the Marquis would not hate her because it was all her fault that he was married.

The Parson blessed them, and as they rose to their feet he said in a kindly voice:

"I shall pray for your happiness."

Then to the Marquis he added:

"You may now kiss the bride."

Ola felt herself stiffen, feeling that perhaps the Marquis would refuse to do such a thing, but he lifted her veil from her face and threw it back over her wreath.

Then as her eyes met his and widened a little in fright, he looked down at her before his lips sought hers.

It was a very brief kiss, more a symbolic gesture than a real kiss, and yet it gave Ola a sensation she had never known before when she felt her mouth possessed by the Marquis and her lips made captive by his. . . .

The Marquis offered her his arm and they walked slowly down the aisle.

Ola, looking up above her where the light of the candles did not reach the shadow of the roof, felt that they were not alone but were being watched by celestial beings who wished them happiness.

When they reached the porch she gave a little gasp of surprise, for outside, lining the way to their carriage, was a Guard of Honour consisting of the sailors from the yacht.

She knew that the Marquis was surprised too, but he smiled as he led Ola through the ranks of his own men, dressed in their smartest rig.

The carriage was no longer closed, and as they reached it Ola saw that the hood was decorated with white carnations like those inside the Church, and the horses had gone.

Instead there were two lines of sailors to draw them, and as soon as Ola and the Marquis were seated they moved off with the Guard of Honour following them.

"Did you know this was going to happen?" she asked.

"I had not the slightest idea," the Marquis replied. "In fact, I thought the only people who knew our secret were the Captain and Gibson."

Ola gave a little laugh.

"I am sure it was Gibson who thought of anything so exciting and so dramatic. It was just what he would enjoy."

"Are you enjoying it too?"

The Marquis's voice was deep and it made her a little shy so that she could not look at him as she replied:

"Of course . . . it is very . . . exciting for me, and how could we have a more . . . wonderful setting for our . . . wedding?"

As she spoke, she looked up at the stars which were now brilliant overhead, and as they drew nearer to the Harbour they could see the moonlight shimmering silver on the sea and the masts of the yacht silhouetted against the whole glory of the Heavens.

The Marquis's eyes were on the rounded softness of her neck as she looked up, but he did not speak and Ola gave him a shy little smile.

"Thank you, thank you!" she said to the sailors as they brought the carriage to a standstill at the gang-plank.

Then as she smiled at them they cheered her and the Marquis, waving their caps above their heads until they had reached the deck and disappeared inside the yacht.

"How can they have thought of such a lovely surprise?" Ola was asking as she went into the Saloon and found that the surprises were not at an end.

There were white lilies standing in huge vases on each side of the sofa and there were lilies on the Marquis's desk, and a profusion of white flowers decorated the table at which they were to dine.

Ola clapped her hands together.

"Who can have thought of anything so lovely?" she asked.

"I will see that everyone is thanked in the most practical manner," the Marquis said with a smile.

She heard him ordering the stewards to serve rum to all the ship's company and for champagne to be sent to the Captain and the other Officers.

It was time for dinner and the Chef had excelled himself in producing a meal that was better than anything Ola had eaten since she had been aboard the *Sea Wolf*.

Finally, when dessert was put on the table, the stewards carried in a large wedding-cake.

"I am prepared to claim credit for this," the Marquis said. "I bought it today when I was choosing your gown."

It was certainly a very impressive cake, of three tiers decorated in the traditional manner with horse-shoes and artificial orange-blossoms, surmounted by a tiny but very French-looking bride and bridegroom under a silver canopy of love-buds.

"We must cut it together," Ola said.

Then she wondered if the Marquis would think that such a demonstration of unity was unfitting.

But he agreed, saying as they rose:

"I should really have brought my sword with me, but I did not think it would be necessary on this voyage."

Ola glanced at him quickly to see if he was talking bitterly, but he was smiling as he handed her a long, sharp knife, saying:

"I am sure, however, that this will be far more effective."

Ola put her hand on the knife and the Marquis covered it with his and once again she felt the strength of his fingers.

They gave her the same strange feeling which she had known when he had kissed her, but she told herself that it was only because she was feeling shy.

The cake was cut, and the stewards, having left two slices on the table, carried it away to offer the rest to everyone aboard the *Sea Wolf.*

A decanter of brandy was set before the Marquis and it made Ola think of the night she had drugged him. As if he was thinking the same thing, he said after a moment:

"We have been through some strange experiences together, Ola, and perhaps the strangest of them has happened today."

She thought he was reproaching her, and after a moment she said in a small voice:

"I . . . am . . . sorry."

He raised his eye-brows.

"For what?"

"Having brought all . . . this about, I know . . . what you must be . . . feeling."

"I rather doubt that."

"But of course I know," she insisted. "You had sworn never to marry, and you told me that you hated women as I hated men, and yet because I . . . forced myself upon you I am now your . . . w-wife."

It was somewhat difficult to say the last word and she stumbled over it because it sounded so intimate.

She felt the colour rise in her cheeks.

"I think we have a great deal to learn about each other," the Marquis said, "and as we are both intelligent people we are both well aware that what we said yesterday does not necessarily apply to today."

Ola gave him a little smile.

"You are being kind to me," she said, "but I want to say something to you."

"What is it?" the Marquis asked.

He had made no effort to help himself to brandy. He was sitting back in his chair, his eyes on her face, and he seemed relaxed, yet almost as if he were seeing her for the first time.

"We are . . . married," Ola said in a small voice, barely above a whisper. "I know it was . . . necessary and there was, as you said, nothing else we could do in the circumstances. But I want you to be happy, and I will do . . . anything you decide when we return to England."

"What do you mean by that?" the Marquis enquired.

For a moment Ola could not reply. She was trying to find words to express the thoughts that were in her mind and yet would not formulate themselves as clearly as she wished.

She said after a long pause:

"If you want me to live . . . apart from you, or if we are together at times because people would think it strange if we were not, I will try to . . . please you and behave in a way that the wife you would have chosen for yourself would behave."

The Marquis did not speak, and Ola, in the light of what she had said, thought perhaps he was considering her suggestion that they might live apart to be a good one.

She glanced at him and thought how handsome he looked and that there was something about him which would make him stand out in whatever company he was in and however many men there were round him.

'He is so distinguished,' she thought to herself, 'and, in a way, magnificent.'

It suddenly swept over her that he was her husband — she bore his name and she was his wife!

Then almost as if a voice from Heaven spoke to her, she knew that she did not want to leave him. She wanted to be with him; she wanted to talk with him . . . to listen to him. . . .

She wanted . . . she could barely express it herself . . . she wanted him to . . . kiss her . . . again!

As the whole idea was so revolutionary, so different from anything she had ever thought about the Marquis before, she felt her heart beating tempestuously in her breast!

In a panic, she wanted to run away from the room in case he should be aware of what she was thinking.

As if he had made a decision, the Marquis said:

"Give me your hand, Ola."

He put out his own as he spoke and obediently she put hers on it and felt his fingers close.

"I think there should be no misapprehensions or misunderstandings between us," he said. "I should tell you now exactly what I want of the future and what I feel about you at this moment."

He felt her fingers quiver as he went on:

"It may be hard to make you believe it, but when we were being married just now I knew it was what I wanted and that you were in fact the wife I would have chosen for myself had we met under different circumstances."

Ola was so surprised that she could only stare at him, her eyes very wide in the light of the candles.

"Do . . . you . . . mean that?" she whispered.

"I mean it," the Marquis replied, "and it is true. Perhaps I should explain to you, although it seems unimportant now, why I said I hated women and why in fact I came on this voyage in the first place."

"No!" Ola said quickly. "No, please do not tell me! I have felt, in fact I am sure, that you have been hurt and wounded and it was a woman who did it, but I would rather not know!"

The Marquis looked at her in surprise and she went on:

"What has happened in the past has nothing to do with me, except that you were there when I needed you most! So if it is possible . . . I would like us to start our life together anew . . . with none of the . . . miseries, the problems, and the . . . difficulties which have happened before we . . . met each . . . other."

She made a little sound which was almost a sob as she said:

"I have called you my Good Samaritan, and that is what you were. If you had not taken me in your yacht when I was . . . desperate, my life would have been very . . . different. It would have been a . . . horror I cannot bear to . . . contemplate!"

"I understand what you are saying," the Marquis replied, "and I think there is no other woman who would be so sensible."

He smiled and it seemed to illuminate his face as he added:

"But then you have always been very original, Ola, and extremely unpredictable ever since we met."

"I know," she agreed, "but I will try, I will try . . . desperately hard, not to do anything . . . outrageous again, but to be quiet and . . . well-behaved so that you will be . . . proud of me."

"I have a feeling that if you tried too hard to alter yourself it might be rather dull," the Marquis said. "After all, I have by this time grown used to dramatics and I have a feeling I might miss them if they were no longer there."

He was teasing her, but his hand still held hers closely as Ola said:

"You . . . know I want to . . . please you."

"Why?" the Marquis asked.

She was surprised at the question and she felt he was waiting for an answer as she said:

"You have been so . . . kind and it is only . . . right that I should want to . . . please the man who is my . . . husband."

"Is that all?"

She looked at him enquiringly, and then because of the look in his eyes she felt her heart beating even more violently than it had done previously.

What was more, it was impossible to look away, and although the Marquis did not move, she almost felt as if his hand was pulling her nearer and nearer to him.

She did not speak and after a moment he said:

"I think, Ola, with your hair it would be impossible for you not to feel very strongly about anything one way or another, and I am therefore asking you what you feel about

211

me. Not as a Good Samaritan or as a wolf, which you told me I was, but as a man and your husband."

Now there was a depth in his voice that made Ola feel as if she listened to music. She felt too that there were vital vibrations passing from his hand to hers.

"What can I . . . say?" she asked a little helplessly.

"The truth!" the Marquis replied. "That is what I want from you, Ola. The truth, now and always. I cannot bear to be lied to."

The way he spoke told her that a woman had lied to him in the past and left a wound that was not yet healed.

Because she had no wish, as she had said, to think of what had happened to him before their meeting, she merely said simply:

"I will never lie to you. But what I feel is difficult to put into . . . words."

How could she describe to him, she asked herself, the feeling she had now in her breast which seemed to be rising into her throat and moving toward her lips?

How could she tell him that she wanted him to kiss her again?

Perhaps he would be shocked that she had such thoughts! Perhaps he would think her fast and immodest, or, in Giles's words, behaving like a strumpet!

Because she was suddenly agitated in a manner which she could not understand, she released her hand from the Marquis's and rose from the table.

"I think . . . perhaps it is . . . getting . . . late," she said a little incoherently. "It has been a . . . long day and I . . . should go to . . . bed."

The Marquis did not move but merely looked at her standing in the centre of the Saloon, her red hair gleaming beneath her veil, the exquisite lines of her figure revealed by the clinging white gauze against which her hands, wearing only the gold ring that he had put on her finger, moved restlessly.

"I am waiting for an answer to my question, Ola," he said.

"I do not know . . . how to . . . reply. I cannot find the . . . right . . . words."

The Marquis rose from the table.

"Words are often quite unnecessary."

He moved towards her as he spoke, and as she looked up at him, very conscious of his closeness, his arms went round her. He pulled her against him, saying:

"Let us express our feelings in a far easier way!"

Then his lips were on hers.

As he kissed her Ola knew that this was what she had wanted, this was what she had longed for, for a long time.

But as his lips held her captive it was impossible to think of anything but the wonder of his kiss.

She felt as if the silver of the moonlight on the sea rippled through her body as the strange sensations that had been in her heart seemed to move from her breasts into her throat and onto her lips.

She was not certain whether she gave the wonder and the beauty of them to the Marquis or he gave them to her. She only knew that they were joined with a rapture that was too perfect to find an expression in any other way.

What she was feeling was love. The love she had thought she would never find.

The Marquis's arms tightened, his lips became more demanding, more possessive, and she wanted to be closer to him, so close that she lost herself in him. She was his completely and was no longer alone and afraid.

He raised his head.

"I love . . . you! I love . . . you!"

The words seemed to burst from Ola's lips.

"That is what I wanted you to say, my darling," he answered.

Then he was kissing her again; kissing her fiercely, passionately, and with an insistence that made Ola know that he dominated her, and yet she was not afraid.

She felt as if her whole body had come alive and she was no longer human but was flying through the sky towards the stars. She was part of the universe and of life itself and very much a part of the Marquis!

'Why did no-one tell me,' she wondered, 'that love is so majestic . . . and so . . . irresistible!'

The sound of the anchor awakened Ola.

As she realised where she was, she gave a little cry of joy.

She was in the Marquis's arms, her head was on his shoulder, and she could feel his heart beating against hers.

"I love . . . you," she murmured.

Then as she looked up to see him in the pale sunlight coming between the sides of the curtains which hung over the port-holes, he was smiling.

"It is . . . true? Really . . . true?" she asked. "I am . . . here in your . . . arms and you . . . love me?"

"Do you still doubt it, my darling?" he asked.

"I thought I must be dreaming."

"You are awake," he said, "and if you have been dreaming about me, then it is true!"

She gave a little laugh which was one of sheer happiness and moved closer to him.

"Were we . . . really married . . . last night?"

"I hope so!" he replied. "Otherwise I can only think, my precious, that your behaviour at this moment is somewhat reprehensible!"

She kissed his shoulder with a passionate little gesture which brought fire to his eyes.

"No-one could be more adorable," he said, "but why did I not recognise the moment I saw you that you were what I had been seeking all my life but thought did not exist?"

"I am . . . ashamed too, of being so . . . unperceptive," Ola said. "But even though you hated women you were kind to me, and as really kind men are few and far between, I was very . . . very lucky to find . . . one."

The Marquis kissed her forehead, his lips lingering against the softness of her skin, before he asked:

"Am I still a wolf in sheep's clothing?"

"A very magnificent, exciting, and . . . demanding wolf, whom I . . . love very much."

The Marquis laughed.

"I might have known you would give me an answer different from what I expected! So let me tell you that I shall be a very ferocious wolf and a very jealous one! If I see any other man admiring your hair or wanting to touch the softness of your skin, I will kill him!"

"There will be no need for you to be jealous," Ola said in a soft voice. "I still hate all men except you, and I love you so much that there is no room for anyone else in my mind, my heart, or my soul."

"And I possess all three?"

"You know you do."

"I also possess your body," the Marquis said, "and it is the most alluring and perfect possession I have ever had."

"Perhaps when you get used to it you will put it on a . . . shelf and . . . forget it."

The Marquis's hands were touching her as he replied:

"I think it is very unlikely, and if I tried to put you on a shelf, my naughty one, I cannot believe you would stay there."

He paused before he went on:

"I think really I am rather apprehensive about what surprises you will have for me in the future. You have already told me that you never repeat your tricks, so I need not be afraid of being drugged with laudanum or murdered by bandits. But there are quite a number of other atrocities in various parts of the world!"

Ola gave an exclamation of sheer indignation.

217

"How can you be so unfair?" she asked. "The bandits had nothing to do with me, and I did save you. Oh, darling! . . . I am so glad I did! Suppose . . . you had . . . died!"

The Marquis pulled her a little closer.

"I am very much alive," he said, "and at the moment determined to make the very best of it!"

His lips found Ola's as he spoke.

He kissed her until she felt the fire that was burning in him light a response within herself which felt like a flame flickering through her body.

She put her arm round his neck, pulling him even closer.

"You are so . . . magnificent . . . so wonderful," she whispered. "Please . . . teach me to love you as you . . . want to be . . . loved."

"I do not think you need many lessons, my precious," the Marquis replied, "so all I want is to teach you to love me as much as I love you."

"How can you love me after the way I . . . behaved?" she asked. "And when did you first . . . think you . . . did?"

"I knew I loved you when you threw yourself in front of me to save my life," he replied. "But before that I found myself fascinated by your looks, by your clever little brain, and most of all by the magic that makes you different from any other woman I have ever known."

Ola gave a sigh of happiness.

"How could you say anything so marvellous!" she murmured.

"As I sat by your bed when you were unconscious," the Marquis continued, "I knew that I wanted to look after you and protect you in a way I had never felt about anyone else. And what was more, I wanted you to stimulate my mind and inspire me, which I never thought any woman could do!"

He smiled as he said:

"Before, I had felt myself completely self-sufficient as a man, but now I know you have so much to give me that is mental as well as physical, and that is something I had never even thought of until now."

"Suppose I . . . fail you?" Ola asked in a frightened little voice.

"You will not do that," the Marquis said positively, "because I believe we were intended by fate for each other, long before we met."

As he spoke, he thought that it was fate which had prevented him almost at the eleventh hour from marrying Sarah, fate which had made him find out about her treachery, fate which had sent him running away as a solution to his problems, and fate which had taken him to The Three Bells in the thick fog to meet Ola.

From that moment, everything that had happened seemed, in retrospect, incredible, and yet fate had meant it to culminate in this moment, when the Marquis knew he was happier than he had ever been or had ever expected to be in the whole of his life.

This was love, yet he had the feeling that he and Ola had only touched the fringe, that there was so much more to discover and to savour.

He had known, when he made love to her last night and made her his, that Ola was different from any other woman he had ever known, and the feelings she aroused in him were not only the rapture of desire but something far more ecstatic and sublime.

Because he loved her he had remembered her youth and her innocence and had been very gentle and controlled so that they had both touched the Divine and become for the moment like the gods themselves.

He felt a surge of gratitude sweep over him because, when he had least expected it, life had brought him the greatest reward that is possible for mankind to have.

A love which is true and perfect!

Then, because the softness and the beauty of Ola aroused him, because his body was throbbing and burning for her, his lips sought hers again.

As he kissed her he knew that she too desired him, and, innocent and inexperienced though she was, she had an instinct that made her respond to everything he asked of her and give him not only what he sought but so much more besides.

"I love you, my darling," he said, "and we will spend our lives finding a happiness that is greater than anything we even thought of or imagined."

"That is the . . . happiness I want to . . . give you," she whispered.

And then as the Marquis took the words from her lips, she felt them merge together into one person.

She knew that the voyage ahead of them towards an indefinable horizon would carry them over an unknown sea that was sometimes smooth and sometimes rough and tempestuous.

But fate had saved them for each other, fate had brought them together. It was also fate which would bring them safely into harbour because their ship was guided by love.